BLOOD AND BULLETS

A TRIO OF WESTERN HORROR NOVELLAS

KEITH LANSDALE
MICHAEL KNOST
JAMES AQUILONE

Book 18 in Crystal Lake's Dark Tide series

Let the world know:
#IGotMyCLPBook!

Crystal Lake Publishing
www.CrystalLakePub.com

**Follow us on
Amazon:**

WELCOME
TO ANOTHER

CRYSTAL LAKE PUBLISHING
CREATION

Join today at www.crystallakepub.com & www.patreon.com/CLP

AMERICAN DEVIL

JAMES AQUILONE

1.

A THOUSAND STREETS and they all smelled of pig shit. Catherine Houlihan knew the stench well from the farm back home in Nebraska. Seven hundred miles away and she still smelled pig shit. She could laugh but she was on the verge of tears as she walked down the gloomy gas-lit streets of Chicago. A damp wind swept across the thoroughfare. The sound of raucous music echoed from inside one of the buildings.

Two drunk men appeared out of nowhere and came rambling toward her. She ran across the macadam as the men laughed at her and pointed.

Her mother, too, would have no trouble laughing at her situation. That condescending cackle that made her feel like a stupid runny-nose child. *Didn't I tell you no good would come from that infernal city?*

When Catherine stepped off the train at the Englewood Station, she'd entered a city of smoke and brick and offal. Buildings taller than anything she had ever seen on the plains of Nebraska. Somewhere not far off something burned. The sickly sweet smell of smoke hung in the air. As Catherine crossed another street, she was nearly run over by a phaeton, the mad driver furiously whipping his two horses. A block away she discovered a woman lying in the gutter, the phaeton driver shouting at the unmoving body that she needed to be more careful. What madness was this place?

The train had been delayed for hours just outside the Chicago city limits. She didn't want to enter the city at night, but here she was. In this alien city, far from home, a city on fire and stinking of excrement. She hurried along, her feet echoing on the wet stone. Every sound, she was sure, came from a thief or cutthroat waiting in the shadows of the next alleyway. She quickened her pace and drew in her thin coat, as another cold blast of air swept off Lake Michigan. Mother warned her about leaving home. "There's nothing in the city but sinners," she'd say. Catherine knew she was right, but sin was better than the pig-shit farm.

She held a crumpled piece of newsprint. Catherine remembered the afternoon when her friend Margaret showed her the advertisement. "WANTED, able KITCHEN GIRL to bake, wash, milk and feed calves; age not under 18." The job posting promised room and board. That's when she decided to leave. That's when she decided to start a new life.

She turned a corner, onto West 63rd Street, and a gigantic sprawling building appeared. It took up an entire block. Three stories high. Squat and dark. Full of blind windows. Finally, after what seemed an eternity of twisting streets, she could get out of the cold and damp, be inside where it was safe and, hopefully, didn't stink.

The word HOTEL was painted in white letters on the window.

But the window was dark, and when she tried to open the door, it was locked. That damn train. She cursed herself—and her mother, for good measure.

Catherine knocked and tried to peer between the rolled-down curtain and the door frame to get a glimpse inside. In the darkly lit room, she saw the reception desk but no one behind it.

Catherine gave another knock and, after a moment, a shadow stretched across the floor. Then the shape of a man appeared. The dark figure approached the door. She stepped back, and when it opened, Catherine began apologizing. "I'm so sorry for arriving so late. But the train . . . "

The man beckoned her inside without a word and Catherine stepped out of the gloomy night.

The inside of the building was empty, except for a scrawny black cat that eyed her warily. A small oil lamp that sat on the reception desk the only light.

The man slipped behind the pine desk. "It's a dollar a day," he said.

Catherine didn't have any money. She was so dumb. The job must have been filled. She could go home. She'd only have to live with the humiliation and taunts from her mother for the rest of her life. Catherine could hear her voice. "*I told you it was a bad idea to leave, didn't I, Catherine? But you never listen to your mother, do you?*"

The man stared at her. He was average looking. Perhaps smaller in stature than average. A big brown mustache and big blue eyes. Even in the dimly lit room, she could see the color of his eyes.

"I'm here about the job."

The man watched her for a long moment. His eyes wide now and welcoming. He said, "The job?"

Catherine held out the scrap of newspaper. "The kitchen girl," she said, trying to hide the desperation in her voice. "I'm over eighteen. In fact, I turned nineteen two weeks ago."

The man smiled, his bushy mustache rising to his nose. Catherine relaxed. It was the first smile she had seen in Chicago.

"Can you start in the morning?"

Then Catherine smiled. "Yes," she said.

"Let me take your bag." The blue-eyed man came from around the reception desk, picked up her valise. "Come. The rooms are upstairs."

2.

T HE ROOM WAS much bigger than she expected, especially for a servant's quarters. The furnishings, too, were more lavish. There was a velvet fainting couch, a walnut dresser with a marble top, and a Persian rug. Nothing like the room she shared with her two brothers and sister in Broken Bow. She prayed for a rug on those cold winter mornings when her feet nearly froze in place because she couldn't find her slippers.

Catherine had little time to enjoy the luxuries. The moment she stepped into the room, a sleepiness hit her. She could barely stand. With half-closed eyes, she placed her thin coat on the fainting couch, and then undressed.

Her threadbare valise, she realized, was on the other side of the room, and she cursed herself. Catherine didn't know if she had the energy to make the short trip. Her body felt weighed down by lead. She thought, for a fleeting moment, about forgetting her nightgown and sleeping in the nude. She had always dreamed of sleeping out in the field *au natural*, a phrase she once read in a fancy book, and feeling the moonlight on her skin. But if Mother had found her, what a beating she'd get. As she trudged across the room, a blast of cold air went up her spine. She grew anxious and the reality of being alone in a strange city overwhelmed her. Her head felt cloudy and her limbs were too heavy to move. She took a labored, wobbly step toward the bed, where her valise lay, but she never reached it.

3.

THE WALLS WERE tight and smelled of dust and mildew. Barely enough to fit a man. But he did fit. He made sure of that. His belly pressed against the outer wall, and he could feel it rising and falling against the plasterboard. He lifted the latch to the peephole and watched the young woman. When he helped her into the room, she'd said her name was Catherine.

She was a tall, sturdy one. Most likely bred on a farm in Iowa, Missouri, or Ohio. Sometimes they even came from as far as Nebraska or Kansas. They didn't need much of an excuse to leave their dreary little lives in some podunk town and come to the newly anointed White City. He couldn't help but think of the cattle in the nearby stockyards. Beside him stood a lever, which he gripped. Certainly, these farmgirls slaughtered a cow or pig without much thought. He pulled gently and his chest expanded. His breath came heavy and deep.

A tiny hiss. And the gas filled the room.

He watched as Catherine wobbled as she bent toward the bed. She tried to straighten herself but only managed to stumble backward. Then she was clawing at her throat and screaming. Her mouth going wide, a giant "O" shape that made her look ridiculous. He couldn't hear the screams. The workmen had done an excellent job soundproofing the room. Perhaps he should have paid them. He chuckled to himself.

The young woman made her way to the door, to escape. He'd counted on that. Where else would she go? Like leading cattle through the chutes to their slaughter.

She frantically pulled at the doorknob. Her strength ebbing away with each pull, but even if she had the strength of ten men, that door wouldn't open. The locksmith also did excellent work. He demanded it. If any of his workmen gave him inferior work, he had them do it again. Or he threatened to ruin their reputations.

She pounded on the door with her fists, no doubt screaming her pretty little head off for someone, *anyone* to open the door. *Please, please, please.* Her back was to him so he couldn't see her screaming. Maybe he could place a mirror on the door so he could watch the next time.

The pounding lessened, fell to a soft rap. The gas worked its way through her respiratory system. Soon the lungs would shut down, and she'd be asphyxiated.

He waited. He could be patient.

She gave one last ineffectual rap on the door. Her shoulders slumped and her head lolled.

Another lever was pulled at the precise moment—it was a fun game, wasn't it?—and a trapdoor opened under her feet. He wished he could see her face then, but he was sure she was already on the other side of life.

4.

CATHERINE DIDN'T KNOW if she was dreaming. Her eyes were closed. She was sure of that. Her eyelids too heavy to open.

Voices. She heard voices. No. One voice. But it was only a murmur. Like someone praying. A chant perhaps.

She wanted to wake up. A terrible dread filled her and she needed to open her eyes.

The murmur turned to a hum. A guttural sound that came from deep within the throat, like the growl of an animal.

In her dream, she saw a man with a long, strange knife standing above her with a dirty grin and small black eyes.

Then Catherine was screaming. She heard the scream in her dream. The scream woke her and she was still screaming as she stared at the same man from her dream. His bushy mustache twitched.

Instinct took control and she shot up from the cold table she had been lying on. She knocked the blade from the shocked man's hand—it clattered on the floor—and she was running.

Catherine flew through the dark cavernous room. The smell of blood and decay filled her nostrils. Candles flickered in sconces deep within the room. She tripped and fell on a heap. As Catherine felt the cold and wet underneath her, she realized she was naked.

She reached out and screamed. A face. She was touching a cold face. Her hand moved over the dry lips and shattered jaw. She screamed again, trying to sit up but falling back on the mountain of corpses. Twisted arms and legs.

The man was coming. His footsteps echoing in the dark.

As her eyes adjusted, she saw a fire blazing in a distant furnace.

The figure stepped between her and the fire. "You are a sturdy one," he said.

The man lunged at her, but he, too, tripped and landed face-first in the heap of bodies.

Catherine ran into the shadows. She was beyond thought, a crazed animal, desperate for escape. She found herself flying through a passageway and up a flight of stairs, and then bursting into the open air.

She kept running, naked, through the cold Chicago streets. Free. Finally free. She never felt more free, even when she left Broken Bow.

5.

"**M**ODERN BLUEBEARD CAPTURED!" blared the newsboys from every street corner.

"House of Horrors in Englewood."

"Dozens of Bodies Found in Chicago Murder Castle; More Victims Possible."

"Who Is Arch-Fiend H.H. Holmes?"

News of H.H. Holmes's capture spread through the city faster than the Great Fire. Every newsie from Arlington Heights to Calumet City shouted his name. They whispered about the butcher of Englewood in the bar rooms and brothels. No one had heard such gruesome tales. Not even in the most sordid penny dreadful.

From the Chicago Globe: *On October 17, H.H. Holmes, aka Herman Webster Mudgett, aged 33, was apprehended by Chicago police in one of the most heinous crimes this city has ever seen.*

Authorities were alerted to the atrocities after one of his victims, one Catherine Houlihan of Nebraska, escaped Holmes's clutches. The woman, aged 17, was discovered running through the streets fully nude when she was stopped by police officer Henry Bostcombe. She told the copper a macabre tale of villainy that led back to Holmes.

For days after the arrest, the city was gripped by the increasingly lurid discoveries that lurked at 611 West 63rd Street.

"Crimes of Holmes Stand Without a Parallel in History."

Investigators discovered seven full corpses and dozens of body parts in the basement of what the papers now called The Murder Castle. Their front pages showed detailed sketches of the cellar's acid bath, crematorium, lime pit, dissection table, and an array of surgical tools. On the second and third floors were dozens of rooms, each equipped with unique devices to kill or torture its victims.

Even more oddly, Holmes offered up a confession and detailed his heinous acts to anyone who would listen. He showed no remorse or emotion in his chronicles.

"Most Appalling Record of Murder to Which Any Man Has Ever Affixed His Signature," read one headline.

Then, just as suddenly as the news broke, he disappeared, seemingly vanished from his cell in Joliet.

"Gone! Accused Villain H.H. Holmes Escapes Prison; Whereabouts Unknown."

6.

"I CAN'T STOMACH these pipe hitters," John "Bathhouse" Coughlin said as he stubbed out his cigar on the brick wall of a nondescript building on Clark Street, among a row of similarly nondescript buildings.

"Though he's unorthodox, he comes highly recommended," Michael "Hinky Dink" Kenna said. Where "Bathhouse" was tall and portly, "Hinky" was short and thin.

"*Unorthodox*, I should say! Come on, Hinky, let's get this over with."

The aldermen descended the stairs leading to the basement. Coughlin gave three raps on the door and a small square window slid open. Two eyes appeared in the hole and blinked rapidly.

"Let us in," the burly alderman said, "before I shut this place down for being a fire hazard."

"Of course, Mr. Coughlin. Of course."

The door swung open and the two aldermen immediately began to choke from the smoke that spilled out.

The Chinese doorman bowed as the men walked past waving their hands in front of their faces. A thick haze lingered in the air.

"Take us to Randall Bond," Kenna said.

The doorman shot a glance at another man, dressed in traditional Chinese garb and a homburg. The opium men stared back with no expression.

"You spoke English just a moment ago," Coughlin said. "You and your opium are a plague on this city, you know? I oughtta cite you all."

The doorman shook his head.

"I'll tear this place apart one room at a time if you don't take me to Bond. I know he's here. He's always here."

The doorman nodded at the man in the homburg, who then led the alderman through the labyrinth of the opium den.

Room after room of men lounging on beds or sofas, smoking

from long thin pipes. No one spoke. No one made a sound. Just bodies and smoke.

"The ward is going to shit," Coughlin said, coughing into his fist.

The doorman stopped in a room that was more dimly lit than the others. He nodded at the two men and left.

A man lounged on a red velvet sofa covered in dark stains. He wore blue-tinted glasses, though he was indoors. He wasn't emaciated but he was close. His clothes hung loosely on his skeletal and lanky frame. His long thin fingers, covered in black deerskin gloves, held a long thin pipe that led to his mouth. Like a baby sucking on a bottle, he nursed on the two-foot-long bamboo pipe.

"Randall Bond, you degenerate louse," Coughlin said, the disgust in his voice palpable, "can you hear us?" He waved the smoke from his face, though it only returned a moment later.

Bond's head drifted toward the aldermen. He took a long pull from the pipe and set it aside. "I never thought I'd see Bathhouse and Hinky Dink in a hop joint."

Coughlin grimaced.

"I know why they call you Bathhouse, but why is he called Hinky Dink?"

"Enough nonsense," Coughlin said. "We're in need of your services, Mr. Bond. And if it weren't a dire situation, we certainly wouldn't be in this den of iniquity. You are a disgrace to your station and this fine city."

"You make an excellent argument, Bathhouse. How could I refuse such a gentleman as you? Yet I must. I won't kill Holmes for you."

Coughlin pursed his lips. "I didn't ask you to."

"But you were."

"I'm not buying that divination garbage. I know what they say about you. You think you're clever, but I wasn't born yesterday. Why else would I be here? The news has been all over the city."

"You're right. It wouldn't take the Oracle of Delphi to know why you're here."

"Gentleman! Enough games," Kenna said. "Holmes is a terror. The longer he's on the loose, the more people who'll die. I don't know how you do it, Bond, and frankly, I don't care. You're the best tracker we have and time is of the essence."

"As much as it pains me, Kenna is right," Coughlin said. "Holmes is a menace. I've been in the same room as that madman and I never want to be within a mile of the fiend again. A darkness burns off his skin. I shiver thinking about it. A human, a rational God-fearing man, wouldn't have done the depraved and wicked things he done. He's in league with the Devil."

"Men do evil enough without the need of the Devil, believe me."

"Evil is evil."

"You'll find him?" Kenna said. "You'll find Holmes? Before he kills again?"

"I can't control what he does. If he's going to kill again, he'll kill again."

"Then the longer you delay, the more lives you are putting in danger."

"What's the bounty?"

"Fifty-five thousand," Coughlin said.

"That's higher than the entire James Gang. You two are serious."

"You've read the papers. Or have you been in this den the whole time?"

"It's an election year, isn't it?"

"Do you want the money or not?"

"I do, but as I said I won't kill him. I'm no assassin. He'll be brought back to Chicago to stand trial. I believe in the law."

"The law doesn't have anything to do with this. This is God's justice. This is ridding the world of evil."

"I *won't* kill him."

"Very well. Find him, bring him to us, and we'll take care of it. I'm no coward."

"I'll need expenses."

"You'll have it."

"That fifty-five thousand will keep you in laudanum for a long time," Kenna said.

"I ought to get up and punch you in the jaw, Kenna." Bond took another pull on his pipe. "For that, you're settling up with Weng before I leave this hop shop."

"Very well," Coughlin said. "But we also insist you take a junior marshal."

"To watch me? I don't use opium on an assignment."

Coughlin smirked. "Or laudanum?"

"You'll need help," Kenna said. "Holmes isn't like any fugitive you've encountered."

"And you're starting now. We have a carriage waiting."

7.

KENNA'S HANDS TREMBLED as he showed Bond sketches from Holmes's Murder Castle. He had already seen images from the newspapers, but these were worse. Stuff even the papers wouldn't print. Bodies without limbs or ears or lips. Half-destroyed faces twisted in agony. But the surgical instruments, dirtied with blood, gave Bond the most discomfort.

He pushed away the images. "I don't need to see this."

The opium had settled in Bond and gave him a sense of security and comfort. The feeling was akin to sitting in a warm bath. The bumpy carriage ride kept him alert and awake, as did Coughlin's incessant jabbering. But the images of the Murder Castle jolted him out of that comfort and returned him to the battlefield and medical tents of Antietam, where he first tasted opium in the form of laudanum, "to reduce his suffering."

"As depraved as the stories the newspapers have been writing, if word got out about what really occurred in that hell house, they'd burn the place to the ground," Kenna said.

"Maybe they should," Bond said.

"Sickens me," Coughlin said. "To think of the evil happening in my own ward."

Bond fought the urge to laugh. Coughlin was the most corrupt politician Chicago had ever seen, and with the city's history of corruption that was saying a lot. Still, Bond didn't worry about Coughlin reneging on his promise to pay the bounty when the time came. Despite his reputation, he had always done right by Bond and the other marshals. Fifty-five thousand dollars was serious money. It would allow him to buy property out west and retire. He'd spend his days with an opium pipe staring at the mountains until he couldn't see anymore.

Kenna handed Bond a photograph of a man in a bowler. "This

is H.H. Holmes, born Herman Webster Mudgett in Gilmanton, New Hampshire."

Bond took the sepia-toned image. Holmes-Mudgett had a bushy mustache and sleepy eyes. They seemed to stare at Bond through the paper. He folded the photograph and placed it in his inner jacket pocket.

"He's a licensed doctor and pharmacist," Kenna said. "A highly intelligent and resourceful man, Holmes has committed every crime imaginable—insurance fraud and swindling, forgery, theft, bigamy, and murder. A fiend if there ever was one."

"An *archfiend*," Coughlin said.

"He's confessed to twenty-seven killings," Kenna added, "but we are positive there are many more."

"Is there no end to his villainy?"

"Where are we going?" Bond asked.

"I am told you have an unorthodox way of tracking fugitives." Coughlin leaned toward Bond. "That you need to be close to the fiend's belongings and surroundings. We're taking you to the scene of the crime."

The carriage stopped at West 63rd.

Bond waited for Bathhouse and Hinky to move, but they stayed put.

"After you, gentlemen," Bond said.

Coughlin shook his head. "You're getting the fifty-five thousand, not us. Besides, we have city business to attend to."

No doubt that business was at the Garfield Park Race Track.

Bond shook his head and stepped out of the coach. "Best of luck at the track," he said.

"Enjoy the basement," Coughlin said, and the coach rattled away.

The Murder Castle. From the outside, an ugly, ungainly three-story brick building used for such banal things as selling pharmaceuticals, jewelry, and candy. Still, even here on the sidewalk, Bond could sense something sinister lurking behind the exterior.

The papers said the building was one hundred sixty-two feet long and fifty feet wide. On the upper floors was a labyrinth of narrow passages, twisting at all angles.

Crowds had gathered, pointing and gossiping. Coppers were stationed around the building to keep out the curious. The first-floor stores were shuttered, closed for business.

Investigators had found the trapdoors and soundproof rooms and secret passageways on the second and third floors. One room was equipped to be filled with knockout gas, Bond remembered reading. Trapdoors on the upper levels opened to chutes that dropped victims to a "macabre facility" of acid vats, pits of quicklime, and a crematorium in the basement.

A burly, mustachioed copper stood outside the pharmacy and nodded at Bond.

"Bathhouse wants me to have a look-see at the basement," he said.

"Yessir. This way."

The copper led Bond into the pharmacy. Shelves full of lotions and elixirs that cured everything from convulsion fits to consumption and bad digestives to piles and rickets.

This was where Holmes spent most of his time when he wasn't torturing and killing. His medical and pharmacology degrees must have come in handy. The doctors Bond had encountered wouldn't think twice about sawing off a leg or spending an afternoon with a corpse. A gruesome lot they were in the medical profession.

They entered a small back room and the copper handed Bond a lantern. He pointed toward a door to his left, which was marked BASEMENT.

"You too?" Bond said. "Another non-coward?"

"Excuse me, sir?"

"Never mind. If you hear a bloodcurdling scream from the depths, ignore it. It's probably just your conscience."

"Sir?"

Bond left the copper, opened the basement door, and descended the stairs. Halfway down, the medicinal smell of formaldehyde and old blood hit him. The security of the opium had completely evaporated now. Invisible worms wriggled over his skin. The walls radiated a dark electricity. He felt as if he was walking into the Ninth Circle of Hell.

At the bottom of the stairs was a long tunnel. Bond held up the lantern and cursed his need for money.

He walked between the shadows, his footsteps echoing off the cement walls. Bond didn't worry about the floor plan. He knew where to go. The evil lured him in like an infernal fisherman reeling in his catch.

A second tunnel doglegged to the left.

Bond felt the shadows gather. The lantern barely enough to fight the immense darkness. He removed his glasses. Whether it was habit or sensitivity, he didn't know, but even in the dim light, his hand rushed up to his weakened eyes. He lowered the lantern and his eyes slowly opened, soaking in the inky dark.

The outline of a room was made apparent.

Though it was lost in shadow, Bond knew the room was large, perhaps taking up most of the block above.

First, he came upon a stretching rack. Bond moved the lantern over the length of the torture instrument, a wooden table with rollers wrapped with rope at both ends. *Holmes isn't like any fugitive you've encountered.* Bond didn't think anyone had encountered someone like Holmes since the days of Marquis De Sade.

Next, he found the acid vat. It had been drained, thank goodness. The papers claimed Holmes used it to melt the skin off his victims and sell the bones to medical schools.

Farther in the dark was a large furnace where Holmes supposedly cremated bodies alive.

Last . . . in the middle of the basement, the dissection table. Here was Holmes's collection of surgical instruments. Despite their diminutive size, the blades and saws and picks gave Bond the worst chills. The glow of the lantern didn't glint off the metal. It seemed to absorb the light, suck it up.

Bond was drawn to one of the tools, a long silver-handled blade. He knew it from Antietam. An amputation knife. Nearly a foot long. Cold and sharp.

How many arms and legs did those knives hack off young men in the surgeon's tents?

Bond began to sweat in the damp basement.

Many had died here, but he didn't feel their spirits. Odd. There were no ghosts here. The place was empty. Only the dread remained. The residue of their pain.

He placed the lantern on the dissection table, slowly removed his gloves, and stuffed them in his coat pockets.

As he reached for the blade, he felt the heat of its energy.

Bond gently lifted it off the tray, gripping the handle with his fingertips. He held it before his closed eyes. Then, with trembling hands, he closed a fist over the handle. The blade burned in his palm, a white-hot heat that snaked up his arm and neck and coiled around his brain. This was the Glowing—a golden light in his mind's eye that expanded until it consumed everything. Leaving only memories.

Bond gripped the blade tighter—the heat fusing the steel to his skin—he squeezed until he could no longer feel the instrument.

The marshal retched.

Blood. Blood everywhere. Geysers of blood bursting from the ground bathing the room in red. The blade slashes across an ivory-white throat speckled with dirt. It feels good. It feels right. Satisfying for the blade to grab the soft neck and slice it open. Red spraying onto the arm of the slasher. The blood like an elixir that gives life to the one spilling it. The blade keeps slashing. Body after body. Piling high on the cold dirt floor.

The golden light in his mind's eye began to shrink, a shadow enveloped it, extinguishing the light. Again, Bond felt that dark electricity and dread. Now it seeped into his skin, and filled him with emptiness. The shadow grew inside him and his knees weakened. Before he fell to the ground, he dropped the blade.

The lantern had overturned beside him, throwing strange shadows across the darkness.

He staggered back to his feet. How many people died here, he didn't know. Dozens, maybe hundreds. He didn't know if the blade was used for most or all of them. He didn't have the strength or the inclination to probe deeper. He might not ever have the strength. The blade was evil, it sat as heavy as a boulder in his pocket, and it had a deep connection to Holmes.

Bond put his gloves back on, quickly picked up the knife, covered it with a handkerchief from his pocket, and shoved it in his coat.

He hurried out of the basement.

Visions from the blade lingered in his mind and mingled with memories from Antietam. It took every bit of strength he had not to return to Clark Street.

8.

O UTSIDE THE MURDER CASTLE sat the aldermen's carriage.

"Get inside," the coachman said.

"Where are the two jokers, Bathhouse and Hinky?" Bond asked.

"Never mind. I'm taking you to Joliet."

"What are the charges?"

"Very funny."

Joliet was forty miles south of the Castle. That's where they held Holmes, not only to keep him locked up, but to keep Chicagoans from hanging him before his day in court. Holmes's stay lasted only two weeks.

As the coach bounced over the macadam, Holmes's knife weighed heavily in Bond's jacket pocket. He had found a leather sheath in the pharmacy, which he used to protect the blade. It gave off a strange heat and shined like a dark beacon in his mind. Bond didn't like it, but he needed it.

The streets were flooded with people and carriages. The usual commotion in the city, which was growing faster than seemed possible. From the street corners, newsies shouted the latest discoveries in the Murder Castle, some real, some pure imagination. The city was too much on the move to slow down for something so inconsequential as a madman.

Joliet appeared over the horizon. It wasn't so much a prison as a penal colony. A twenty-five-foot-high limestone wall surrounded the complex. Its twenty-four buildings housed murderers, rapists, and arsonists. Two thousand of the city's ugliest souls.

The warden, a mousy man with a slick mustache and thick glasses who looked more like a bookkeeper than the head of a prison, stood outside the main building, a wide imposing brick affair.

When Bond got out of the coach, the warden shook his hand and said, "You're that queer marshal they think can find Holmes?"

He said it with no animosity and Bond didn't take it with any ill will.

"Coughlin said you'd be coming, though, I don't know what you could find in his cell that would give you any indication of his whereabouts. We have been over it with a fine-toothed comb."

The warden ushered Bond into the building. It was a quiet place and somber. The only sound was the echoing footsteps of staff in the hallways. The warden stopped before a strong-looking guard with a scar running down his right cheek.

"Mr. Gustason will take you to Holmes's cell."

"Right this way, sir," the guard said, and led Bond through the hallways of the main building until they were outside and within the compound.

"That Holmes was a strange bird," the guard said as they crossed the campus, heading toward a building that looked like a proper castle with turrets and towers. Holmes must have felt right at home. "Liked to write letters. All day writing letters. Then you know what 'e went and did?"

The guard waited for an answer.

"No," Bond said.

"'E ripped 'em up? A looney if you ask me."

They entered the prison house. Gustason nodded at the man at the front desk, and then he took a ring of keys off his belt and opened the steel gate door. Inside was a long row of cells, but the guard stopped at the first one.

"We kept 'im close to keep an eye on 'im. You always wear 'em strange glasses?"

Bond stood outside the cell. The ceiling was low, just a few inches above his head, and he could touch both walls if he stuck his arms out.

Another clatter of keys and locks, and the cell swung open. Bond removed his gloves before entering. The guard watched him closely, finally quiet.

The cell could barely fit its cot. In the corner was a bucket, no doubt the privy, and nothing else.

Bond stood beside the cot, which had a flimsy mattress, pillow, and thin gray blanket. "Has any of this been changed since Holmes escaped?"

"No, sir, it's just as he left it."

Bond stooped a bit and ran his hand over the blanket, and then lifted it and touched the mattress. He straightened, a look of disappointment on his face.

"You sure the bedding wasn't changed?"

"Absolutely, sir."

He touched the walls, and felt nothing but the cold and damp stone.

"Would you like to touch me?" the guard said, and laughed.

"As soon as I'm done I'll touch you where the sun doesn't shine." The guard pursed his lips. "I'm done here. This was a waste of time."

"I should say so, sir. You are a most unorthodox marshal."

"People keep telling me that."

"Holmes is most likely hundreds of miles away. Probably murdering women in New York by now."

The guard stepped aside as Bond exited the cell. Bond grabbed the bars of the door to close it, and froze.

His eyes rolled up into his head and a flame of heat shot from the metal, into his arms, and filled his body. A chaos of images crowded his brain.

A prairie. A desert. A plain. Scrub and cactus. Heat. An endless blue sky . . . Holmes is heading south. He'd been thinking about it for a while. In his cell, making plans. He has family . . . No. Not family. Property. He has land down south. That's where he's going.

Bond pulled back from the bars.

"What in God's name was that?" the guard asked, making the sign of the cross.

Bond came to his senses. The guard stared at him like he was a freak. He supposed he was.

Bond stepped away from the cell and put his gloves back on.

The guard locked the door. "You may be a looney, too."

"As looney as they come. Just how did Holmes escape, if I may ask?"

9.

LIKE EVERYTHING ELSE with Holmes, his escape was a mystery. One morning, he had simply vanished. His cell was still locked and no one knew where he had gone, or they weren't talking. No one recalled seeing him outside his cell. Holmes, like many of his criminal ilk, had the power to charm. He had beguiled countless women to their deaths. It wouldn't have taken much for him to sweet-talk a guard.

Or perhaps, Holmes didn't exist any longer and Bond was searching for a phantom.

The coachman had one more stop. A horse ranch in Lockport, just north of Joliet.

"They'll fix you up here," the coachman said, and tossed Bond a good-sized leather purse that jingled when he caught it. As the coach drove away, Bond opened it and found a small fortune in silver dollars. *Bathhouse must have done well at the track.*

The ranch manager outfitted Bond with a few days' worth of supplies and a fine-looking Saddlebred.

Bond was fixing the saddle to the horse when a Mexican with a big smile approached him. He led a black and white Appaloosa.

"I'm Navarro," he said. "Coughlin sent me. I'll be riding with you."

Bond hopped on top of his horse. "I told them I work alone. I don't need a nanny."

"They already paid me, Mr. Bond. I could use the money." Navarro smiled wide, revealing several missing teeth.

"Then take your money and enjoy it. I'd recommend a good dentist."

Navarro laughed heartily. "That's funny. I like you already."

"I've wasted enough time. Holmes is already two days ahead."

"I'm a good scout. I can help you."

Bond spurred his horse and she bolted.

"How do you know where Holmes is heading?" Navarro shouted after Bond, but he kept going.

Navarro hopped onto his horse and set out after the odd man.

The Mexican kept a slow and steady pace. If he had to track Bond, he would. After a mile, he pushed his horse into a lope, the wind whipping his face. He continued on, along the Des Plaines River, leaving the city and what seemed the last remnants of civilization.

10.

THE YOUNG GIRL stared at the queer man in the top hat. He looked familiar, but he wasn't one of the men who worked at the lumber yard with her father or a member of their church. She studied his hands. They weren't rough like those men. His nails were neat and clean. Like a woman's.

She turned away as he looked up and pretended to stare out of the train window. "Miriam Josephine, what is with you?" Her mother elbowed her gently in the ribs.

"Mother, please," she said softly. Miriam stole a glance, but the man in the top hat wasn't looking at her. Thank goodness. He was reading a newspaper now and she couldn't see his face.

He didn't like this. Something was wrong. The girl staring at him, her eyes searching, her mind reaching for the answer to a question. She saw his face on a wanted poster. That was it. The police certainly found the gentleman's body by now. He needed money and clothing. Slipping out of Joliet was easy enough. The big Swedish guard's greed was enough for Holmes to manipulate. A promise of riches for securing him inside a barrel. Once the teamster had been a few miles from the prison, Holmes jumped out of the wagon. On the road, he chanced upon a gentleman wearing a wool frock coat and a top hat. With a rock, he bashed in his head, took his clothing, a cane adorned with a silver serpent's head, and twenty dollars in cash. The coat was a bit large, but that was fine. He hid the body as best as he could in the bushes beside the road. He was usually more careful disposing of bodies, incinerating or melting them. Or selling them to the medical college. There had been no time for subterfuge. Or cleverness. He prided himself on how careful he was. The plans. The double and triple checks. Then the farm girl destroyed it all, years of secrets spilling out after one terrible night, and now he was a fugitive. He needed to get as far away from Chicago as he could. The train was the quickest.

The young girl with the harelip craned her lovely smooth neck. The audacity of it. She was too stupid to hide her curiosity. Her neck was long and soft and white. His blade would cut through the soft skin like tender pork.

His favorite blade was gone. Left behind during that infernal night when everything changed. A stupid girl who couldn't just die. This one was stupid too. And her stupidity was going to lead to more trouble. But he had another blade. The gentleman probably thought he was clever with his hidden dagger in the shaft of his cane. When the time came for him to use it, he faltered, too slow to protect himself.

Now the girl with the harelip was talking to her fat mother, who was looking at him too. The fat woman's eyes grew large and now she was pointing. The others around her looked as well, and whispered to each other. They all seemed horrified, clutching their chests.

Holmes reached up to his cheek. It was wet. He wiped his skin and looked at his fingertips. Blood. Not the escaped girl's. This came from his eyes. Blood trickled from the corners like red tears.

Holmes folded his paper and rose from his seat.

Women cackled behind him. Excited voices and shifting bodies. He didn't turn.

Calmly he made his way out of the car.

Holmes flung open the cabin door and was greeted by the roar of the train engine and the clatter of the iron wheels on the tracks and the wind rushing past him. He scurried across the gap and jumped into the next car. This car was sparsely occupied. He looked for a seat far away from the others, especially curious little girls.

He dropped into a seat toward the back and watched the scenery roll by the window. They must have been close to St. Louis by now. He was anxious to leave Chicago. The city never grew on him. Too crowded. Too many eyes. Too many looky-loos.

The car door flew open and a ticket agent stood scanning the room. He knew that look.

The fat woman now stood behind the agent. She was pointing at him. A scowl on her face. She seemed to be saying, "That's him."

Holmes stood calmly and walked toward the back of the cab. He heard the agent's feet hurrying toward him. He slid open the door, the roar of wind blasting him.

"Sir, wait! Sir!"

The agent slipped through the door as it closed. Holmes stood with his back against the entrance to the other cab. The agent stumbled into the opening, and as the door banged shut behind him, Holmes leaped across the gap, pulled the dagger from his cane, and slashed it across the agent's throat. His eyes bulged as thick spurts of blood splashed Holmes in the face. Before the agent could scream, Holmes clamped his hand over the man's mouth and began to lap the fountaining blood from his wound. He tore at the ragged flesh with his teeth and swallowed it. When he was done, he pushed the limp agent onto the rushing earth below.

He'd have to abandon the train. It was foolish to think he could travel among the public. They'd be looking for him everywhere. He had to be smart. Stealthy. Stick to the shadows.

He watched the landscape rush by. The world a blur.

He placed the dagger back into the cane, tossed it in the grass, and then tossed himself after it.

He landed on his side and rolled a good distance away from the tracks, eventually crashing into a bush.

The train rattled away into silence.

He sat up. Nothing was broken.

He dusted himself off, stood, and trudged back to the tracks in search of his cane.

11.

"**Y**OU CAN'T SEE real good, can you?" Navarro said. He'd caught up with Bond just before sunset. Bond had camped along the river and made no effort to conceal his fire.

"I see well enough."

"Can I sit down?" the Mexican asked as he hopped off his Appaloosa. He didn't wait for an answer. He secured the horse to a tree and sat on the other side of Bond's fire. "It was quite easy to track you."

"Stop patting yourself on the back. If I wanted to be lost, you'd never find me."

Navarro took a strip of jerky from his breast pocket and tore off a piece. "You are a queer one. Do you have eyes in your head behind those odd glasses? You do realize the sun is nearly down? I knew a man who just had empty sockets in his head. Had some disease that ate away at his eyes till they disappeared. Damndest thing. Funny for a tracker to be blind."

"I'm not blind."

"Do you ever take off the glasses? It makes people uncomfortable, like you're hiding something."

"Are you uncomfortable?"

"Perhaps a little."

"I'm sensitive to light."

Navarro searched the dimming sky. "What light?"

Bond saw in his mind's eye the canister exploding before him, nearly blowing off his head. The world going white and silent.

Navarro laid on the ground, took off his jacket, bunched it up, and used it as a pillow. "And what about the gloves?"

"You ask a lot of questions."

"I am a curious man. I have another, if you don't mind. How do you know where Holmes is heading?"

Bond stirred the fire with a stick. "I don't know where he's going, just a general sense of his direction."

"They said you're the best tracker in the Midwest, maybe in the country."

"I don't know about that."

"Wasn't it you who brought Wildman Jack in last summer? He had evaded capture for twenty years, living in the mountains. What's your secret? Maybe I can become the second-best tracker." The Mexican smiled his missing-tooth smile.

With Navarro's words, the blade grew heavier in Bond's pocket. He had forgotten it was there. How had he forgotten? He pulled open his overcoat and pulled out the leather sheath. He placed it in the dirt beside him. Bond felt lighter without the blade, but the desire to pick it back up and have it next to his skin was strong.

"What's that?" Navarro jerked his head toward the sheath.

"Something I found in Holmes's basement."

Navarro eyed Bond. "A souvenir?"

"A key."

"Pretty big key. Why do you think Holmes does it?" Navarro asked, watching the river. "Kill like that?"

"Why do men hunt or gamble or race horses? For the thrill of it. He enjoys it. It might be the only thing he enjoys. It's bloodlust. A compulsion. He'll never stop. Not until he's in the ground."

"But the aldermen said you won't kill him."

"Not in cold blood. Killing Holmes isn't my job."

"I'm told you don't carry a firearm."

"Don't have a need for one."

The Mexican chuckled. "You're the first marshal I ever heard say that." Navarro removed a revolver from his side holster. "I'd never track without my Colt. If I get the chance to kill him, I'm taking it."

"Is that why the aldermen sent you? To kill Holmes?"

Navarro followed a piece of driftwood as it rushed down the river, toward the sinking sun. "I don't know why the aldermen sent me with you. Maybe they thought you'd get lonely."

12.

SOMEWHERE AROUND SPRINGFIELD, they spotted the bodies.

They had started out just before dawn, the blade back in Bond's coat pocket, pressed against his side. At first, it hung heavily, but now it felt light and wasn't even noticeable. Several times he had to pat his coat, fearing it had slipped out. He thought of the laudanum in his satchel. It had been a while since he tasted its oblivion.

The trail turned a hard right around a stand of trees. Bond and Navarro reared their horses and took in the horrific sight.

A man, tall and husky, possibly in his thirties, swung from a tree. His shoes were missing. A girl, no older than fifteen, lay naked on the ground directly underneath the man's swaying feet. Her abdomen had been cut open, her innards spilled out onto the dirt. A vulture sat on her chest, its face buried in her wound. Bond dismounted, picked up a stone, and hurled it at the ugly bird. He missed, hitting the girl's thigh, and the vulture continued snacking on the fresh guts. Navarro, still in the saddle, drew his Colt and shot the damn thing, which gave a terrible squawk and fell on top of the body.

Bond jumped at the sound of the gunfire. "Put that damn thing away, you idiot!"

"Where's the blood?" the Mexican said, as he got off his horse. Panic in his voice.

Bond bent next to the girl. Her glassy brown eyes stared blankly into the sun. He closed her eyelids. A piece of flesh had been torn away from her neck.

The blade seemed to shiver in its sheath. A warmth radiated from his pocket.

Holmes did this. Bond was certain.

He removed the glove on his right hand and placed his fingertips on the girl's cold and pale arm.

His head bent back and his body shuddered.

The girl and the man are riding in a coach. It stops on the trail. After a moment, the coachman yells. Then there's a shotgun blast. Suddenly, a man with large blue eyes set too close together enters the coach and orders them out.

"The devil," Navarro said, breaking Bond from his vision. "The devil walks among us. This is blasphemous. There's no blood. Look in the dirt."

Bond put his glove back on and stood. "Holmes did this."

"You can tell from just touching her?"

"Help me get him down." He nodded at the hanged man.

"If Holmes did this, he must be close. Let's go."

"Get him down! We're burying both of them now."

"There's no time."

"I'm not going anywhere."

Navarro fired three times at the noose, severing it and sending the body crashing to the dusty ground.

Bond punched Navarro, his fist connecting to his jaw, the Mexican stumbling to the side and nearly falling into the corpses.

He rubbed his jaw and then laughed. "You have no problem using your fists, do you?" The Mexican looked at Bond. "I could shoot you dead."

"I don't think you will, Navarro. That's not who you are, even if you think you are."

"You're pushing me, amigo."

"Help me to dig."

They dug for hours. It was sundown before they buried the bodies in shallow graves. Navarro crafted makeshift crosses and stuck them in the dirt.

"When we get to town," Bond said, "we'll let them know about the bodies and they can take care of this."

13.

MATILDA RUSHED FROM the garden once she heard the stomping hooves and snorting. A man sat atop a carriage driven by two huge black stallions. The horses were the largest she had ever witnessed. She could barely see over their backs.

"Sorry if I startled you," the coachman said with a bright smile. "They are intimidating looking, but believe me, they're big puppies."

"Are you lost?" Matilda asked.

The man looked tiny and a bit silly inside a dusty coat at least two sizes too big. Matilda relaxed some, but her mind was on the shotgun inside the cottage. It was right next to the door. Matilda was pretty sure she could run inside and get it before the man even dismounted.

"Is it that obvious? I'm afraid I am. I've been starving all day so I thought I'd take a shortcut and find an inn or restaurant, but I hadn't found anything until I stumbled upon your lovely cottage."

"I'm afraid you'd have to go to Springfield twenty miles north of here."

"Wrong direction for me, I'm afraid. My horses can use some feed if you have any. I can pay."

The man reached into his coat pocket and pulled out a handful of silver dollars, some of which spilled out of his hands and clattered to the ground.

"Certainly. Where are my manners? You can leave the horses and carriage beside the house. I'll fix you lunch."

"You are too kind. It will feel good to get off the road and rest for a minute. It's been a trying day."

Matilda went into the cottage while the man drove the carriage to the side of the house. She was probably being overly cautious but she grabbed the shotgun and moved it into the kitchen. A woman alone couldn't never be too careful.

She had fresh bread and plum pudding. Matilda put the food out on the table and then put wood in the firebox for coffee.

The man still hadn't knocked at the front door. Matilda wondered what was keeping him. She went to the door and looked out. The back of the carriage sat beside the house. Matilda was about to call out for the silly man in the big coat but thought better of it. She turned back to the kitchen to get the shotgun, and the man was standing behind her.

"How did you get in—"

The man's hand flew out and swiped across her throat. Matilda fell back, grabbing at her neck, wondering why it was so wet. Then the man was lunging at her, his face red as fire. She screamed but there was only a burning silence.

Holmes lathered his face in front of the mirror. The straight razor still dripped with blood. He watched the liquid splatter in fat drops onto the dresser. The blade must have been the husband's, but the man was nowhere to be found. Perhaps she was a widow, which would explain the razor's dullness. It was rough going but it did its job.

In the mirror, he saw black tendrils, like inky spider legs, swim in the whites of his eyes, and then disappear. Holmes ran the razor over his cheeks, replacing the frothy lather with the woman's blood. The blade stuttered over his cheek, nicking him. He hacked at his thick mustache, gouging his upper lip, his blood mingling with the woman's. The sweet substance ran over his lip and into his mouth. He closed his eyes and remembered the screams. The flash of the razor. The satisfying catch of the blade edge into the smooth skin and the parting of flesh, like the opening of a window curtain letting in the sun.

The woman lay, facedown, on the bed behind him. Naked and pale.

It was a small cottage, neatly kept. Seemed a lonely existence. Out here, isolated, and away from others. No man to keep her company or protect her. A shame.

He needed a place to rest and recoup, figure out his next move.

The train was a mistake. For too long, he lived anonymously. But now the veil had been lifted. Holmes ran his hand over his smooth cheeks and felt the blood drying on his skin.

The husband's clothes fit better. He found pants and shirts in one of the drawers. The coat he took from the fat old man in the coach was even bigger than the one got from the gentleman.

He sat on the edge of the bed, next to the woman of the house. She was like all the rest, fighting to the end. He appreciated her strength as he ran his hand over her cold back.

He could stay here, settle down. Tend to the garden. It was a nice idea. But there was so much farther to go. So much more to be done before he could stop.

The number was one thousand and one thousand was the number. It rang in his head. *One thousand souls.*

How many had it already been?

Not enough. Not nearly enough.

He went to the kitchen to eat the meal the woman had prepared for him, and then he'd take the coach back out on the road.

14.

BOND AND NAVARRO set out in the gray of morning. They followed a trail through hilly country, the trees going bare. Bond's bones creaked in the saddle. He was still sore and tired from digging. He knew it slowed them, but he'd be damned if he'd let those poor souls rot on the road.

Navarro stayed silent all that morning, which Bond appreciated.

In the afternoon they camped in a field to give themselves and the horses a rest.

Bond took off his jacket and placed the sheathed blade under it.

Navarro made coffee over a fire before dropping down on a log with a newspaper he got back in Peoria.

"They discovered more bodies," the Mexican said. "*Children's bodies found moldering.* They found the remains of two little girls in the cellar of a house Holmes was renting."

"Can't you read something else?"

"It helps me to nap."

"Just close your eyes."

"What do you see when you close your eyes, Bond?"

"More than is dreamt of in your philosophy, Navarro."

"Shakespeare. I'm an educated man, you know."

"But not a believer?"

"I believe in God. I don't know if I believe in *you*, Bond."

Bond laughed. "Hand me something of significance to you."

"One of your carnival tricks?"

"Whatever you care to call it. If it's not of significance, I'll know."

Navarro grabbed his satchel, opened it, and removed a coin. He handed it to Bond.

Bond placed the worn silver coin on this knee and removed his right-hand glove. Navarro watched with interest. Bond held the coin in his bare palm for a long moment. He smiled and flipped the coin to Navarro.

"She must be worried about you," Bond said as put his glove back on.

Now it was Navarro's turn to smile. "I don't know who you mean."

"Milagros, but everyone calls her Millie."

Navarro stopped smiling. "How did you know that?"

"Carnival trick. Nothing more." Bond shrugged. "*As long as you hold this coin, you hold my heart.*"

Navarro's eyes got wet and he choked up. "I must talk in my sleep."

"No hard feelings about the punch? I didn't mean anything by it."

Navarro rubbed his jaw. "I barely felt it, amigo."

Bond dozed off and dreamed of The Murder Castle and bathing in Holmes' acid bath, his skin sizzling like bacon in a grease pan.

15.

THEY RODE INTO town just before sunset. Nothing more than a Main Street with a saloon, general store, church, and ironsmith.

No one was at the livery stable, which was next to the saloon. Bond and Navarro put their horses in stalls and tossed in some hay. They figured they could sort things out in the morning.

"Let's have a drink," Navarro said. "Or do you not drink?"

Bond sat at the bar. Navarro sat next to him.

The barmaid leaned against the other side of the bar, her head resting on her fist. She didn't seem interested in the two dusty men who entered the saloon.

"Do you have rooms?" Bond shouted at her.

She didn't look up. "Does it look like we're busy?"

Bond didn't need to look around. The place was empty.

"Give us two rooms."

"One dollar, payable now."

"And two shots of whiskey."

Bond put two silver dollars on the bar and watched the barmaid shuffle toward them. She reached for the whiskey, poured the shots, and placed them in front of the men.

"To our patrons, Bathhouse and Hinky!" Navarro said, and downed the whiskey.

Bond threw back his glass and slammed it back down on the bar.

The barmaid scooped up the coins. "You two are the first customers I've had all week. This town is deader than Lincoln."

"Speaking of the dead, there are two bodies we found on the road," Bond said. "We buried them about forty miles back along the main trail. Let the sheriff know. He might be able to identify them and get them back to any family they may have."

"No sheriff in these parts. He left with the rest of them when the mine dried up about a year ago. I'm just waiting for my husband to return from back east and we'll be gone too."

"Are there any officials around here?"

"There's a priest. Father Mulaney."

"If you could get word to him, I'd appreciate it."

"Sure thing. Was it redskins?"

"No. Give us another round."

The barmaid poured more whiskey and the men drank.

When they were done, the barmaid led them up a flight of stairs to their rooms.

Navarro bid Bond a goodnight, put a coin in the barmaid's hand, and disappeared into his room.

Though Navarro was growing on him, Bond was happy to be alone. He could think better. He pulled back the window curtain to let in the moonlight. He didn't bother to light the lamps.

He placed the blade on the dresser and unsheathed it. It felt heavier than before, a burden to carry. He was happy to no longer have it on his person. The object had an odd pull on him. For some reason, he had the urge to pick it up, slash someone's throat, and lap their warm blood.

He took off his coat and removed his glasses.

He stared at the blade, not knowing why.

In his satchel was a small bottle of laudanum. Bond didn't lie to the aldermen about not taking it when he was working, but he always carried a bottle. In case.

He placed it next to the blade.

Bond thought the blade and laudanum were different things, but they both held him in thrall. He understood why the laudanum held him. But the blade? They both called to him, but the blade was louder. It wanted to be held, to be used. Objects contained a spirit, he knew. They held on to their owner's vibrations. Sometimes an object can be haunted, take on a life of its own. He felt the pull of the blade the first time he touched it.

He could learn a lot from that piece of metal and he feared the awful wisdom. He feared its power over him.

Bond removed his gloves, flexed his hands.

He had touched haunted objects before. They weren't pleasant. But this was different. It *wasn't* unpleasant. It felt good. It felt right. Like the laudanum. But stronger. More all-encompassing.

Black thoughts swirled in his head, warm, soothing thoughts, lowering him into an inviting abyss . . . and before he knew it, he had touched the blade. Just a quick tap. He pulled back his hand. A jolt of lightning went up his arm. Holmes's grinning face flashed in his head.

He rubbed his burning finger.

Bond sat in a chair in a corner of the room, away from the blade, his heart thumping.

Sleep was far away. He could have used more whiskey, but he didn't want to move. He was rooted in the chair.

In the dark, he remembered.

. . . the air seems filled with bullets. A storm of lead. Balls and canisters shrieking, whistling, hissing in the godforsaken sky. A shell strikes a horse, bursting it to pieces. A shell explodes nearby, shrapnel lodging in my face. The world goes black.

. . . the field hospital at Antietam. Worse than the battlefield. The dead and wounded are gone. But their arms and legs lie in piles in the bloodied dirt. Many of the amputated limbs still wear boots. Hands stick out of shirt sleeves. Feet dangle from empty pant legs. The smell of blood and rotting flesh.

. . . a clearing in the woods beyond the battlefield. We rest on a log. Patrick and I. To talk, to rest. Patrick makes a joke. I laugh. At that moment, a rifle cracks in the valley and my mouth fills with my friend's brains.

. . . the hand grenade, hurled by a rebel. Rolls to my feet. Before I can run, it explodes and the world falls silent. Blind in the hospital. The only sounds are screams and young men sobbing for their mothers. When my sight returns, I could see another world.

Bond stared into the darkness.

The night was long and they had many more miles to go. The laudanum would plunge him into much-needed sleep. This was for the best. He would be no good without rest.

He put the laudanum to his lips and drank.

To sleep. To stop the memories. To stop the past.

He undressed and fell into the bed, his head spinning and heavy. Sleep came quickly.

Again, his dreams brought him to the basement of the Murder Castle. This time, he was strapped to a metal slab, naked, in the middle of a dark room. He couldn't move, couldn't speak, though he tried. His throat straining to make a sound, the littlest squeak, but it was no use. With every ounce of strength he could muster, he tried to move, but he was impotent.

Something moved among the shadows. Bond knew it was coming for him.

Holmes appeared above him, looking down at Bond like he was a bug. A smile. Holmes held up the long blade. All shiny and sharp and dangerous.

Bond screamed in his head.

He could hear someone drowning in one of the acid baths as their skin melted away. Then the sound of the saw on flesh and bones. He thought of Antietam. Always Antietam.

Holmes lowered the blade and slid it across his chest, drawing blood.

Then Holmes slashed Bond's throat and he awoke, chest pounding.

He sat up in the darkness and wondered if he had screamed in his sleep. He waited for Navarro or some other guest of the hotel to bang on his door, but there was only silence. He felt foolish. The laudanum made him drowsy and his thoughts foggy.

In the corner of the room, appeared a dark shape.

Holmes.

He felt his presence.

Bond leapt out of the bed, landing unsteadily on his feet, and headed for the blade on the dresser. The laudanum slowing him. Holmes was faster. He grabbed the silver-handled blade as Bond crashed into the fiend.

Holmes fell back against the dresser and Bond nearly dropped to the floor.

He recovered and swung wildly. Bond jumped back, but Holmes sliced his arm. Blood poured from the wound, and Holmes watched it with lustful eyes. Bond walloped Holmes in the jaw. The killer staggered into the wall.

Bond was on him, grabbed Holmes by the shoulders, and he froze. A white-hot heat snaked up his arms and the world turned golden. Something twisted in his brain, something alien. The same pull when he touched the blade. He felt the thing try to wrap itself around his brain. Black thoughts wormed their way into his brain.

The darkness calling to him, wanting to consume him.

He fought the urge, pushed the thoughts away. When his eyes

opened—he didn't even realize his eyes were closed—Holmes was running out the door.

Bond took two steps and fell to the ground, his head spinning.

He staggered to his feet and rushed out of the room, barefoot and in his long johns.

Holmes flew down the stairs like a phantom.

Bond had to steady himself against the wall as he made his way down to the saloon. The laudanum still had its hooks in him.

When he hit the bottom of the stairs, he froze. Bond didn't know if he was in a laudanum dream or not. The barmaid's body was sprawled out on the bar. Her stomach ripped open, her innards spilling out and dripping to the floor. Her arms pinned to the bar top with large knives. Her throat slashed open, her head at an odd angle. Her eyes staring blankly at the ceiling.

The saloon doors swung to and fro. Holmes was gone.

Bond grabbed one of the knives staked into the barmaid and ran into the cold night.

Holmes was a hundred yards ahead, heading out of town. Bond no longer had Holmes's blade, but he still sensed it, knew where it was going, where Holmes was going. He ran barefoot over the dusty terrain, his breath blowing smoke into the air, blood spilling from his arm.

Navarro. Where the hell was he? He must have heard the tussle next door. Why hadn't the damned Mexican come? Bond knew he was a no-good waste. He didn't need him.

Bond found himself deep in the woods, and he was back in Antietam. The bullets whizzing through the air, the cry of battle, explosions. He closed his eyes and covered his ears. When he opened them again, he was back in the present.

He came to a field, a clearing, and there he found Navarro.

The Mexican screamed, but it quickly turned to a whimper. He was suspended, tied between a tree and a pair of monstrous black colts with red eyes and clouds of smoke pouring from their nostrils like smoke from a chimney. Holmes stood behind the horses, one hand on the farthest colt's rump. Thin streams of blood ran from the maniac's eyes like tears. He gave the horse a soft pat, sending both horses slightly forward, tightening the ropes and stretching Navarro. He screamed in agony.

"Take another step, marshal, and I send these two to Mexico and they rip your boy in half."

Bond stopped.

Navarro moaned, his arms and legs pulled tight.

"Let him go, Holmes. You can't escape."

The fiend laughed. "It's you who can't escape. I'm free." Holmes threw open his arms.

"You have the blade. Isn't that what you wanted? Let Navarro go."

Again Holmes laughed, a high cackle that boomed like the rifle shot that blew his friend's brains out.

"Why are you doing this? What's the point of all this evil?"

Holmes grinned, the same grin from his dream.

"Evil? What do you know of evil? I will show you evil, the wicked hand that guides me. I will show you a place where there is no fear or pain, a place where you will be free. Not Heaven or Hell, but right here on this Earthly plane. I will free you, Bond, but like the rest, you must suffer. Suffering is the best teacher."

Holmes hopped onto his colt, gave the command, and the two devil horses bolted.

Navarro screamed as his body tore in half. A sickening sound. The colts flew through the night like wraiths, dragging Navarro's torso along the rocky ground. His screams quickly faded into the midnight sky.

Bond watched the infernal sight, unbelieving. He shouted, "Navarro!" and then gave chase. Bond stumbled and fell on his wounded arm. He yowled. Not from the pain but in frustration.

He was a fool. He'd never catch Holmes on foot. He rushed back to the hotel, now feeling the cold and the rocky ground below his bare feet.

How had Holmes found him? How did Holmes even know Bond was hunting him? The blade. It connected them. He was reminded of something he read . . . *If you gaze long into an abyss, the abyss also gazes into you.*

He didn't need the blade to find Holmes anymore. He was no longer connected to the blade. He was connected to Holmes now. And he knew where the fiend was going.

Fort Worth. He had property there. A new Murder Castle.

Bond gathered his things from the room. Fortunately, Navarro's revolver was still in his room. Bond took it.

He couldn't waste time burying the barmaid. He could hear Navarro's voice protesting. Instead, he laid the barmaid behind the bar and placed a tablecloth over her.

He left the saloon and headed to Texas.

16.

BOND SOLD HIS horse in a town called Rolla in Missouri. Now that he knew where Holmes was going, Bond decided to take a train to Fort Worth, which would save him days.

As they rolled into Joplin, Bond read more stories about Holmes. The entire country, it seemed, was obsessed with the butcher from Chicago. They were even calling him the American Ripper.

SECRETS OF THE MURDER CASTLE REVEALED!
TICKET AGENT BELIEVED TO BE HOLMES'S LATEST VICTIM
CRIMES OF HOLMES STAND WITHOUT A PARALLEL IN HISTORY

Randall Bond believed in things most other men didn't. He hadn't always been a believer, but he had seen things, experienced things. Bond had never encountered anything like Holmes. That bastard Hinky was right. If there was ever true evil, it was inside H.H. Holmes.

Holmes came to Bond every night in his dreams, but it was no longer Holmes. His nightmares were haunted by a shadow, a malevolent force without a name that stalked Holmes, and hungered for his soul.

Bond drank the laudanum to sleep. He had little choice.

Bond got off the train in Denison, Texas, a boomtown that bustled with activity. He found a hotel at the edge of the city, among the brothels and gambling halls.

He bought a Mustang from a Cherokee and rode it out to the Red River.

He hitched the horse to a tree, took out his bottle of laudanum, and placed it on a boulder. He got Navarro's Colt, stood about twenty-five yards away from the rock. It had been decades since he held a gun, but it felt like only yesterday. After the war, he couldn't bear the sight of a firearm.

When he returned home to Pennsylvania, Bond learned that his wife and son were gone, killed by a rogue band of Confederates who had raided their town months before. If he had a gun at the time, he would have used it on himself. Of that, he was sure.

Bond stood, lifted the Colt, and fired at the glass bottle. The gun crackled and Bond's hand flew up, nearly hitting him in the face. The shot pinged off the rock.

Bond removed his right glove. He gripped the Colt and could feel Navarro's spirit inside the revolver. It was a welcome relief from Holmes's blade. He shouldn't have been so hard on Navarro. He was a good man. He could feel it in the gun handle, a brightness, a warmth.

He fired again and this time he hit the laudanum dead center, shattering the glass and spilling the liquid. He kept firing at the shattered glass until his hand no longer flew back. He wondered what Navarro would have said.

Bond needed to be ready for Holmes. He'd stay in Denison for as long as he needed.

His dreams of Holmes or whatever the shadow thing was intensified. It spoke to him in a language beyond language. He felt its words, its meaning. It invited him to escape, promised freedom in abandon.

On his third night in Denison, Bond realized it was music. It was the language, too, of the opium and laudanum. The song of escape. The voice sang to him every night, sang him to sleep. Deep into the darkness of oblivion, where nothing can reach you and nothing exists. The bottom of the universe. Far from everyone. Buried under the world. The womb of existence. The song of annihilation. Forever alive and never alone. In darkness's cold embrace. Bond shivered in the Texas heat. Saw only darkness in the star-gleaming sky.

Where was God in all of this? Where was His voice? Bond didn't hear it. With all he had seen, never once did he see God or feel Him. The Glowing only brought him to the dark heart of the universe. The darkness of this land. Filled with ancient blood.

The memories of his dreams haunted his waking hours. As Bond rode to the Red River, he heard the echoes of the song. The land hummed its tune. And his horse galloped to its rhythm. Bond's heartbeat fell in rhythm and it all felt like one rotten organ, inside the body of a mad god.

In the town, he'd pick up bits and pieces of the continuing horror being unearthed in Chicago and beyond. Holmes had cut a bloody swathe from New England to Philadelphia to Chicago. Now he planned to expand his fiendish reach. Every new detail another blow to civilization.

17.

BOND LEFT DENISON on a blazing hot morning. He rode south across the plain under a cloudless sky that stretched to the end of the Earth. He pushed the Mustang into a lope, and then spurred him into a gallop, driving him faster and faster. With every mile, he felt his draw to Holmes strengthening. The darkness spreading and enveloping him. As if he was caught on a lure and being reeled in. In his mind's eye, he could almost see Holmes. His shadowy shape lurking on the edge of his vision. All the while, the siren song played in his head, getting louder and louder.

Bond checked into a hotel. He needed to gather his strength. It had been a long journey and he wasn't the strongest of men. He needed to be smart, too.

He had steak and coffee for dinner. It was a struggle to get it down.

Bond kept seeing Navarro's torso being dragged along the dirt. The demonic stallions, eyes blazing, puffing clouds of smoke from their flared nostrils.

He had to push all the images from his mind if he wanted to finish this job.

That night, sleep came to him easily.

In the morning, Bond set out for Rusk Street & East 2nd Street.

18.

BOND HAD NO doubt he was correct about the second Murder Castle. The building on Rusk Street & East 2nd Street was the mirror image of the Chicago castle. A peculiarly constructed, imposing three-story building with wooden bay windows, and storefronts on the first floor and two stories above for his other activities. He had no doubt there would be a stone basement, too.

For all its depravity, the first Murder Castle was only a prototype. The new den of iniquity would be his—*its*—crowning achievement. Bond shuddered at the thought.

As it was in Chicago, the new Murder Castle was just three miles from the stockyards. The smell of offal and slaughter always in the air. Holmes felt at home next to the abattoirs. His killings part of a process, his victims nothing more than livestock.

Bond had the same foreboding feeling that he had in front of the Chicago Murder Castle. A sinister presence lurking behind its walls. The building a living thing with a rotten heart.

The street was deserted. Perhaps the citizens of Fort Worth knew enough to stay away.

Bond hitched his horse to a post on the corner and grabbed a lantern he brought along. The storefronts lacked signs and products in the windows. On closer inspection, they were empty inside, without shelves or counters. The building was waiting. It had an air of expectation. Ready to be filled with products and people. Victims for Holmes.

Scaffolding was erected on the southern edge of the building. The new Murder Castle was still under construction. That gave Bond some heart. It wouldn't be at full strength.

Bond checked the doors or any point of entry.

The entrance to the hotel did have a sign. The words HOTEL

painted in thick white paint on the glass.

This time the door was unlocked. Of course.

Every step of the way, he felt as if he was being pulled inside. He knew the devil had his hooks in him and he allowed it. Did he have a choice? It didn't matter. He needed to face Holmes. End this one way or another. He owed that to Navarro.

He felt the weight of Navarro's Colt in his pocket. He hadn't fired a gun at another human being since the war. Would he hesitate?

He lit his lantern and entered the building's darkness.

A musty smell. Fresh paint and sawdust.

The inside was identical to the one in Chicago. A small room with a pine reception desk. Bare wooden floor. Holmes planned to recreate the horrors of Chicago here. Do it all over again. Create another factory of suffering and death.

Bond removed his gloves and touched the reception desk. The wood smooth, newly shellacked. He got no reading. No spark, no Glowing. Bond suspected the second Murder Castle hadn't seen any death. Or was that wishful thinking? Holmes was readying it, preparing, and soon it would be churning out bodies as readily as the nearby stockyards.

If this was a copy of the Chicago castle, then Bond knew the second and third floors were where Holmes's depraved games started, in the various rooms of gas and fire and spikes. And they ended in the basement. That den of horrors below ground that held the bones and blood.

Bond knew he was playing Holmes's game. But he didn't have to play by his rules. He mounted the stairs, holding the lantern in his left hand and the Colt in his right.

Bond had read the stories about the Murder Castle and quite frankly hadn't believed them at first. He had no such doubts now.

What kind of mind could construct such rooms?

From Bond's memory of the Chicago Castle, the second floor had six halls, thirty-five rooms, and fifty doors.

The floor, like the house itself, was a labyrinth of passageways and rooms.

Atop the stairs was a short hall. To his right was a closed door. Bond gripped the doorknob, held it for a moment—it was a dead piece of glass. Locked. He turned left at the end of the hall. Four more closed doors, two on each side and another left turn. Bond placed his palm on the doors but got no readings from either. All locked. Ahead was a tight passageway, another left. Bond squeezed through and found another door. A dead end. This one was open. Holmes was guiding him in. The song whispered in his ear and it sang . . . *Come* . . .

The room was empty save a door to his left. Bond knew that many rooms couldn't be entered unless by way of another room.

If he went any farther, he'd end up in a gas chamber or fall into a trap door leading to the basement. He hoped his senses would alert him to any danger. He reached out with his mind, opened the door, and found a large room. A wooden box sat in one corner, a large hose ran from its top and snaked to the middle of the room, unattached to anything. That was the asphyxiation box. Holmes put his victims inside and filled it with gas. Fortunately, it wasn't finished. Bond thought better than continuing through the labyrinth. The pull was great. The darkness tugged at him, and he wanted to go. The song grew louder, clearer.

Come . . . come . . . come . . .

Bond's heart hammered to a strange rhythm.

He turned to leave the room and that's when he heard a voice from somewhere deeper in the castle.

"Bond . . . Bond . . . Dear God."

A finger of ice ran down Bond's back.

Navarro. But how?

Was Holmes playing more tricks?

"Marshal . . . Please."

Navarro was still alive?

Bond swept through the asphyxiation room and bounded into the next . . . through blind rooms and empty rooms . . . up to the third floor.

The top floor was unfinished. The rooms had not been built. Wooden frames had been hung here and there. But one stood complete, in the center of the floor.

The door ajar.

"Bond . . . Please."

The voice louder.

Bond held up the Colt and the lantern.

He crept toward the door. His mind racing with a million possibilities. His hands wet with sweat, his muscles stiff.

Bond pushed the door open, his gun held at the ready.

He wasn't prepared for what he witnessed.

Navarro was, indeed, still alive. Impossibly.

His torso had been strung up from the rafters by chains. His lower half, of course, was gone. His innards kept in by a hasty cauterization. The skin black and ragged.

Navarro screamed. His mouth spewing blood with every vocalization.

"Navarro? How?" Bond uttered.

"Bond . . . Please . . . kill me."

As Bond rushed toward Navarro, the door slammed shut behind him.

Blood dripped onto his head as he reached up to the junior marshal, who never should have come on this infernal journey. Bond cursed Bathhouse and Hinky.

Navarro was too high up. Bond couldn't reach him.

Navarro reeked of rotten meat and fear. Bond could feel the terror wafted off him like smoke.

Bond searched the room for something to elevate himself so he could reach Navarro, who had gone limp and silent.

"Navarro, stay awake! I'll get you down."

But it was too late. The knockout gas had already filled the room.

Bond passed out underneath Navarro, his blood dripping onto his cheek.

19.

THE GAME BEGAN on the second floor and ended in the basement.

Someone hummed in the dark.

Bond's eyes fluttered open. Vile breath, warm and steamy, hit his nostrils. A crazed face smirked. Big blue eyes. Scarred cheeks. The mustache was gone but it was undeniably Holmes's face.

He hummed a broken tune. The same song Bond heard in his head.

He was naked, strapped to a table. Strong leather straps held down his arms and legs and head. Bond tried not to think how this paralleled his nightmares. He attempted to move but was held in place, a bug staked to the ground.

Holmes stood over Bond, candlelight flickering in the recesses of the dank basement. He made tiny cuts in Bond's chest with a scalpel, drawing pearls of blood.

Deeper in the basement, Navarro moaned. A low cry of agony.

This was Hell and Holmes was the Devil.

Something black wriggled in Holmes's eyes, like tiny worms.

"The basement doesn't feel like mine. It doesn't fit," Holmes said, his rank breath warming Bond's face. "It's the little things. The air isn't right. Dry and hot. I prefer the Chicago chill. The cold in your bones that makes you pull your coat tighter, snug like a bug in a rug."

"Why are you doing this?"

Holmes cackled.

"You hear it, don't you? The bees in your head. I can see it in your face. They buzz all day. Buzz, buzz, buzz. But at night. At night they sing. More like cicadas. They've been singing to me ever since I was a little one. I used to tell my mother I must have swallowed a bee. She didn't believe me, of course. But that's how the Devil entered my body. I had no control over it. There's no use fighting Him. The dark nights, thinking and thinking. Black thoughts that turn to black actions. The Devil is more powerful than you and I. Believe me."

Holmes made another cut in Bond's chest, pressing the scalpel into his skin until it popped through.

Bond winced, though relieved it wasn't the amputation blade.

"It helps to make holes," Holmes said. "It's not hurting, is it? Don't be such a child. They're only small cuts." Then his voice got rougher. "I can make much deeper cuts, if you like. Much deeper. You will scream for eternity. It's a long fucking time."

His voice returned to normal. "You and I are not that much different. They sang to you and you came. Something sang to the farm girls and they just kept coming and coming. From Kansas and Nebraska and Oklahoma. I couldn't keep up."

Holmes cut another hole in Bond's chest. The blood mingled with the other cuts.

"I'm a doctor, you know? I hold several degrees. It happened when I was dissecting a corpse. He was an old man. Shrunken from age and death. Wisps of white sprouting from his liver-spotted head. His skin was thin and the scalpel cut through it like paper. That I remember. How easy it was. Unlike my fellow students, I enjoyed the work. I had plenty of practice. I would find small animals—squirrels, possums, rats—and cut them open in the woods. Lay out their parts on the ground. Sometimes I'd try to put the organs back, but it never fit. Isn't that strange? The old man, I didn't even know his name. I cracked open his ribs and cut a Y-shape down to his pelvis. Gently folded back the skin. I don't know if you'd call it his soul or not, but a force, a spirit left his body. There was a spark. A flash. Blinded me for a moment. And that force entered into me. I felt my lungs fill and my blood boil. My brain ran wild with a million thoughts at once. From that day on, the voice spoke to me. It has never left me."

Holmes dropped back into the shadows of the basement. Bond's chest heaved. The blood dripping down his sides.

When Holmes returned, he held the amputation blade. Bond's heart froze and he felt his bowels ready to release.

"You have only yourself to blame. You could have brought help. A posse to round me up. But you work alone, don't you? You'll never be alone after today."

Holmes laughed like a maniac. It was clear he was out of his mind.

"You'll be free soon. I don't want to hurt you. I didn't want to hurt anyone. Ever since the day the dark spirit entered my soul. I remember it well . . . it happened when I was twenty-one sitting by the river . . . when a snake came along . . . "

Holmes held up the long blade, which looked as if it had doubled in size.

Holmes opened his mouth and stuck out his tongue. A smirk. And then he swung the blade, lopping off his tongue . . . which flopped onto Bond's chest. Bond let out a scream. Dark, thick blood poured from Holmes's mouth, a big grin spreading across his crazed face.

"What in God's name are you doing?" Bond yelled.

Before he knew it, Holmes shoved the writhing tongue into Bond's mouth and clamped it shut. Bond's eyes bulged, felt as if they'd explode from his skull.

The tongue waggled in his mouth. He fought it, but he couldn't move his head. And Holmes's hands were like iron. The tongue crawled to the back of his mouth. Bond couldn't breathe. Then it was down his throat, Bond gagging.

Holmes pulled his hand back, and Bond screamed.

With the amputation blade, Holmes cut away Bond's restraints as he cackled and grinned and jabbered on senselessly. He freed Bond's legs and arms, but before he could cut away the strap from Bond's head, Bond kicked himself off the table, sliding his head out of the strap, and barreled into Holmes, who fell back into the stone wall of the basement. Bond leaped upon the man, who gave no resistance. He continued his choked cackling as blood dripped from his tongue-less mouth. Bond punched him in the jaw. Holmes's head twisted to the side and slammed against the stone. Bond raised his fist again, but Holmes raised the amputation blade and Bond backed up.

Holmes tried to speak but managed only to gurgle blood. He looked at Bond with blazing eyes and plunged the amputation blade into his own neck. Holmes yowled like an animal. Then he pushed the blade farther into his throat, blood spraying, until he slumped to the ground, motionless.

Bond kicked Holmes but he didn't stir.

Navarro moaned.

Bond went to him.

The twisted torso writhed in pain. Navarro had been propped up against the back wall of the basement. His eyes closed, his head lolling on his shoulder, he said, very low: "Kill . . . me . . . please. End it."

Bond didn't know where the Colt was. It would have been cleaner. He went back to Holmes's body and picked up the amputation blade, the handle hot and wet. As Bond made his way back to Navarro, the buzzing began in his head. His skull had turned into a beehive.

Navarro moaned.

"I'm sorry, friend." Bond swiped the blade across Navarro's throat, cutting his head clean off. The head dropping to the ground and rolling into the shadows.

Bond watched as the red liquid spurted out of Navarro's severed throat like an awful geyser.

His stomach clenched.

The bees sang and he listened to their song. The music, he now knew, had been playing since before the first pyramid, given voice by a god transformed into a demon.

Bond dropped to his knees and began lapping up the sweet-tasting blood from Navarro's neck.

One thousand souls, the voice sang in his head. *You owe me one thousand souls and then we will both be free.*

THE DEADWOOD DEAL

MICHAEL KNOST

CHAPTER 1

MOVING CRADDOCK'S HORSE out of one stall and into another, Jack gently stroked the Appaloosa's neck. "Don't get all jittery on me, girl. I'm just gonna shovel out your space so you'll have more room to do your business."

Manure and leather and straw lingered in the air, all the things he'd become accustomed to the past few months at the ranch.

"'Course if I ate as much as you, I'd be shittin' myself out of the barn as well."

The horse flicked its tail and quietly followed Jack's lead without resistance or hesitation.

"McCall."

It was downright spooky how Lucian Craddock could sidle up on a fella without a sound. "Need you to go into town for supplies," he said, holding out a scrap of paper. "Here's the list."

"All right." Jack examined the handwriting that looked more like chicken scratches than letters or words.

"You *can* read, can't ya?"

"'Course I can read!" Jack hastily folded the paper as heat gathered in his chest and neck. "You and the ranch hands all think I'm some sorta idiot or something. Well I ain't, ya know!"

Craddock's wiry eyebrows converged at the bridge of his nose. "Boy, you *ever* take that tone with me again and I will cut that blamed tongue right outta your mouth." His eye twitched. "We clear on that?"

Jack nodded, the warmth spreading throughout his chest.

"Second of all, there ain't nobody here who thinks you're an idiot." Craddock's expression softened. "You're just a young'un is all—makin' the same mistakes every one of us made at your age."

The warmth advanced into Jack's cheeks and ears.

"Now get on into town and fetch them supplies like I asked."

He gestured toward the horse. "You can finish things up here when you get back."

"Yessir."

"Better take the buckboard . . . some of them items will be a mite cumbersome."

Hitching the mule to the wagon, Jack kept his eye on Craddock as he left the barn just as quietly as he'd entered it. The grizzled rancher may have been a bit long in the tooth, but Jack remembered the old cuss beating the piss and vinegar out of a strapping young cowhand who'd somehow crossed the line.

"I'm gonna show 'em all one day, Jasper." The mule's ears perked up, twitched. "And they're gonna go on about how they knew me 'fore I made a name for myself. Just you wait and see."

The ride into town was a rough one in spite of the road's well-worn ruts. Jasper held a slow enough pace, all right, but the wagon somehow rattled and banged the entire way.

Craddock had gone on the past few days about getting a wheelwright to grease the axles and check the spokes, but decided against it when he learned the town's blacksmith could do the job cheaper. All Jack knew was the dang contraption jarred his guts almost as badly as that cantankerous bull the ranch hands coaxed him onto a few weeks back. The laughter still seared his conscience.

Stretching out like an ocean of crops and red Quinlan soil, the Kansas plains may as well been the surface of one of them planets Doc McDowell always went on about when compared to the Kentucky landscape Jack's family called home. The absence of mountains and hills was downright homesickening—it just wasn't natural to be able to see as far as one's eye could actually behold.

It seemed as though Doc McDowell knew a little something about everything. In fact, Jack's pa referred to the old man as the limey-know-it-all because he was always going on about planets or moons or the time he lived in a fancy railcar for several months . . . all in that fancy British way of speaking.

Maneuvering Jasper next to several horses in front of the saloon, Jack scanned the area for movement. The ruckus of laughter, music, and drunken revelry emanated from the establishment's batwing doors, where a tinny piano melody kept everything in some sort of chaotic rhythm.

Climbing off the wagon, Jack hitched Jasper to a post with several branded horses, something he'd only witnessed once in life.

"Well I'll be."

Tobacco smoke reached his nostrils, reminding him of his old man. Several months had come and gone since he'd gotten word that James McCall had been killed in Abilene.

Pushing through the doors, Jack found the saloon exactly as his ears pictured it. Tables spread out across the rough-wood floor with a few patrons playing poker and drinking. Others were in conversation and drinking. And some . . . well, some were just drinking.

A cold breeze washed over him as he located the gang at a table in the corner. Must have been seven of them, but he figured a few others were more than likely milling about with the regular crowd, keeping an eye out for anyone seeking to catch them by surprise. But those at the table were the big dogs. And right there in the middle of them all, just as big as life, was none other than Butch Carver.

Keeping his gaze fixed on those at the table, Jack made his way to the bar. No one gave him a second glance as he waded through the crowd, paying close attention as to not bump into anyone or jostle a table.

"What'cha want, boy?" The proprietor didn't bother looking up from the whiskey glasses he was stacking under the bar top.

"I have a right to be here as much as anyone!"

Glancing at Jack, the man shifted a cigar stump from one side of his mouth to the other. "To *drink*." He shook his head. "What'cha want to *drink*?"

Grunting, Jack scanned the bottles on the wall behind the portly man. "Just give me a whiskey. Somethin' cheap."

He slid a coin across the counter and knocked back the hooch in one gulp. The burn slithered into his throat and chest.

"Best take it easy on that rotgut, fella. It'll sneak up on you like a pissed off rattlesnake if you're not careful." Butch Carver moved next to Jack, holding up two fingers for the bartender.

"Ain't that the truth. But a rattlesnake will at least give you a warning 'fore it strikes."

"Sounds like you've been bitten a time or two." He handed Jack one of the freshly-loaded glasses. "Name's Butch Carver."

Taking the whiskey, Jack stood motionless. "You don't remember me."

"You know, every time somebody says that, I end up defending myself over something I did or said—or at least something they *think* I did or said." He dropped his hand close to his sidearm.

"Just a minute." Downing the liquor, Jack held up his empty hand. "I didn't mean it that way at all." A chill tingled up his legs. "My old man used to run with you fellers a ways back."

Butch cocked his head, squinted. "Good lord almighty, are you Jimmy's boy?"

The bright queasiness in Jack's chest softened. "I wasn't sure if any of you would recognize me."

"To be fair,"—Butch held up two fingers for the barkeep again—"you was just knee-high to a grasshopper the last time I saw you."

"You fellers gonna be in town a spell?"

Handing Jack another shot, Butch shrugged. "Hard to say." He knocked back his drink and grimaced. "Now *that's* snakebite good right there," he said, gesturing toward the empty glass.

Jack downed his own. "Much obliged for the drinks."

"Hey." Butch thudded Jack's chest with the back of his hand. "Come over and let me introduce you to the boys."

The crowd parted as Butch made his way toward the gang's table. Jack followed through the collapsing Red Sea of revelers.

"Guys." Butch put an arm around Jack's shoulders and offered a shifty grin. "Does this fella remind you of anyone?"

"My god, Butch, you let on like you've single-handedly sired every sombitch from here to Nacogdoches." The man tried to hide his gap-toothed grin before boisterous laughter overtook the others.

"Just doin' my part to replenish the earth, Henry," Butch said, joining in the laughter. "Just like the good book instructs."

"I think you overlooked the part where the Bible says you ain't s'posed to do that with your *neighbor's* wife!" Henry's face reddened from cackling.

Jack forced a smile, moving his gaze from Butch to the gang and back.

"Some of you were around when this fella was just a tyke. Anyways, this here's Jimmy's boy."

Henry rose to his feet. "I never would have guessed it in a thousand years." He took Jack's hand, shaking it. "Your old man was one of the best—as loyal as they come."

"Well I'll be roostered," the tall, black man said, getting to his feet. "I'm the one that made that slingshot for you when you was but a mere pup." He removed his hat as if standing graveside, paying respects. "Your pa was always goin' on about you and your sisters."

"Are you Elijah?"

"You gots a good memory!" His smile dampened. "We lost a good man when we lost your pa."

"What exactly happened to him?" Jack tried conjuring an inkling of spit in the desert that was now his mouth. "I know he got shot and all, but I never heard any details of who did it or why."

Butch retrieved his arm. "That burden is for those of us who was supposed to have been there for him."

Henry picked up a whiskey bottle. "He deserves to know the truth, Butch. After all, it's his pa we're talking about."

"It's too much for him to carry." Butch motioned toward Jack. "He ain't one of us, Henry. He ain't *like* us." He shrugged. "And what good is it gonna do him anyways?"

"It's his—"

"He'll end up getting his fool self killed!" Butch grasped Jack's shoulders. "Look, kid. When we find the bottom feeder who did it, you can rest assured *we'll* make him pay."

Jack dropped his gaze to his boot tips. "I may not *be* one of you fellers, but you ain't got no idea as to whether or not I'm *like* y'all."

Butch grinned. "Sounds like something Jimmy would have said."

"So if none of you was there when it happened, then how do y'all know who did it?"

"We got the culprit's description from somebody who *was* there," Henry said, prompting a glare from Butch.

"So you're saying you don't really know *who* did it, you just know what the guy looks like."

"Well, to be honest"—while still speaking to Jack, Henry eased his gaze to Butch—"there are a bunch of men who fit the description."

"So you're saying—"

"Listen, Jack." Butch removed his hat, wiped his forehead. "The details we gathered could describe at least a half-dozen men in this saloon at this very moment: tall, long hair, mustache." He shrugged. "There's more, but I don't want to take a chance on you going over the deep end every time you see someone with that depiction."

"You know, Butch, we've been in need of another gun since Jimmy's death." Elijah gestured toward Jack. "Maybe he could take his pa's place."

"That's not a bad idea." Butch leaned forward as though searching for some kind of fire in Jack's eyes. "How would you like to be part of the gang when we catch up with your father's killer?"

"You serious?"

Butch smiled. "You got a horse?"

Jack jutted a thumb over his shoulder. "Back at the ranch."

"Better go fetch it. We need to brand that beast if you're gonna ride with us."

CHAPTER 2

"WE'LL CAMP HERE." Butch climbed off his horse and pointed toward the landscape. "These rock formations will make good cover."

Stirring dust finally caught up with them, silently passing among their ranks like spirits of the past, oblivious to the here and now.

"Let's gather some firewood," Henry said, tugging Jack's arm.

Darkness moved in, stretching shadows across the scorched earth. Most of the trees and vegetation looked to have been dead for years without a single drop of rain.

"Where we headed?" Jack picked up a few broken branchlets. "Nobody's said nothin' about anything."

"We got a job in Wyoming."

"Doin' what?"

Henry broke a limb across his knee and cradled the pieces in one arm. "Hunting buffalo for the railroad."

"Buffalo?"

"Yep. Quick and easy money." He paused a moment. "You seem surprised."

"I just expected a little more . . . lawlessness, I guess."

"Being on your own out here is dangerous." Henry snapped a twig for demonstration. "Truth is, we band together for protection." Bundling several twigs in his grip, he feigned a failed attempt of breaking them. "It's not about being outlaws, it's about improving our chances of survival."

"Funny how that worked out for my old man."

Dropping the branches, Henry grabbed Jack by the lapels. "Don't you be spoutin' off with a bunch of malarkey you know nothin' about!" The words came through a smattering of gnashed teeth. "Your pa was more family to many of us than our own flesh and blood."

"I didn't—"

"Yeah, yeah." Henry shoved Jack away and started retrieving the scattered wood. "You'd best keep that foolish talk to yourself. And just so you know"—he aimed an unwieldy bough at Jack's chest—"*Shedding* blood with someone is just as much kinship as *sharing* blood with them."

"Honest, I meant no offense."

Henry stared at the ground a moment before finally moving back toward camp. "This should be enough to get the fire started."

"Henry?"

"Yeah?"

"Did Pa kill anybody?"

Henry looked as though he'd just took a swig of clabbered milk. "Now why would you go and ask something like that?"

"Just curious is all." He rubbed the back of his neck. "Pa never talked about his work . . . or you fellers, for that matter."

"Well if Jimmy'd wanted you to know any of that stuff, *he* woulda told ya himself." Shifting the tree limbs in his arms, Henry started toward camp. "Let's get some vittles rustled up."

The campfire crackled and popped as heat and flickering light ebbed and flowed in the darkness.

The grub was warm, but that's about the only positive thing Jack could say about it. The beans were bland, the coffee was stale, and the hardtack was nothing short of barely-edible rocks. But the men didn't seem to be too put off with any of it.

"You gots a gun, Jack?" Elijah had that bewildered look on his face again—the same look he always had while seemingly in deep thought.

"I lost the only one I had a few weeks back in a poker game."

"Lord have mercy." Elijah rummaged a grimy saddlebag. "Here," he said, handing over a Colt Single Action Army. "I'm returning the favor in your pa's honor."

"I can't accept this."

Taking Jack's wrist, Elijah forced the weapon into his hand. "It be the least I can do." He sat back, nodded. "After all, Jimmy gave me my first one. And besides, you'll be needin' it."

Jack opened the revolver's loading gate and gently rotated the cylinder. "I had no idea you were in the army."

"Not me." Elijah chuckled. "No sir, I acquired that piece from a genuine enlisted fella."

"So . . . you stole it?"

His eyes grinned as broadly as his mouth. "Now you knows it ain't polite to kiss and tell!"

The weight and feel of the revolver was comfortable in Jack's hand—almost too comfortable. "Thank you."

"Best keep it in an oiled rag or somethin' to make sure it's good and protected. Last thing you want is it jammin' up on you when you needs it most."

Flipping the revolver over, Jack scrutinized the grip. "How long did you know Pa?"

"I'm guessin' right close to fifteen years or so." His bewildered expression developed into a sneaky grin. "That old buzzard saved my hide the very night I met him in Kansas."

"Really? What happened?"

"I was waitin' on a freight boss to finish up some paperwork in town." He raised an eyebrow. "Couple a drunken mudsills accused me of lookin' at 'em crossways or somethin'. 'Fore I know'd it, I was starin' straight down the barrel of a six-shooter."

A faint breeze washed over them, carrying light embers and smoke.

"Then this big fella walks up and puts a gun to the ear of the man pointin' his'n at me." Shaking his head, Elijah grinned. "Jimmy cocked back the hammer and told that fella, 'Go right on ahead if you feel froggy, son . . . but just you remember, frogs with glass asses only jump but once.'"

"Pa said that?"

"He sure did." Elijah slapped his leg and laughed. "Hard to say who was ready to mess their britches more, them mudsills or *me*!"

"What'd they do?"

"Them boys tore off down the way like scalded dogs." He shrugged. "I bought your pa a few rounds of whiskey and he invited me to ride with him and Henry."

"So that's . . ."

"That's how we got started."

Jack stared across the campfire, watching the flickering shadows contort and warp Butch Carver's face. "You reckon he'd teach me how to quick draw?"

Elijah followed Jack's gaze. "You mean Butch? To be right

honest with you, I don't think he knows *how* to draw fast, I think he just can."

"Ever seen him draw on somebody?"

"More than *one* somebody." He turned back to Jack. "Different folk have a God-given talent for stuff. They don't learn it, they just does it." He shrugged. "I know'd a shopkeeper in Kansas who could remember *everything* he read . . . word for word. That fella remembered every bill of sale, every inventory list, and every single number on a tally sheet." Shaking his head, Elijah grinned. "It was like he was readin' those pages and numbers right from his naked brain."

"I ain't never heard tell of anything like that."

Elijah motioned toward Butch. "*His* talent is killing men 'fore they can kill him. He can draw and shoot straighter and faster than most can blink. To be real honest about it, I don't think that's something anybody can teach."

"Maybe." Jack pushed a smoldering log deeper into the flames. "But he just might be able to offer some advice on getting started."

"Come take my rifle, Jack." Butch's whispers were nearly lost in the wind as a dozen or more ambling buffalo grazed just down the hillside. "I want you to focus on that one right there." He gestured toward a specific cow to the left. "That's the leader."

"How can you tell?"

"Just do as I say. We'll stay downwind of the herd, getting as close as we can without spooking them." He put a hand on Jack's forearm. "Tell me what's next."

"I'm gonna drop the leader first, and then I'm gonna take my time picking off those around it—one shot, one kill each."

Butch nodded. "Don't forget, you're going to *squeeze* the trigger, not pull it or yank it like you did earlier."

Crouching as they moved, the two men inched quietly ahead while Elijah stayed behind on the hillside. The bison's pungent muskiness overwhelmed them the closer they approached.

"I don't think—"

Putting an index finger to his lips, Butch surveyed for movement, and then motioned toward the lead cow. "Do it," he mouthed.

Perspiration trickled around Jack's eyes, threatening to blur and sting. *You can do this.*

"Remember, ease your breath out while *squeezing* the trigger."

Jack put a bead on the behemoth and made an effort to clear his thoughts from the thundering heartbeat in his ears.

You can do this.

The blast caught him by surprise as the recoiling buttstock rammed into him, sending pain to his shoulder and the Winchester to the ground.

Reaching to retrieve the rifle, Jack fell forward and recognized the panicked movement from the bison.

"Move!"

Just as he caught sight of the lead cow barreling down on him, Jack grabbed for his hat while Butch drug him away from the imminent impact by his collar.

Another gunshot roared with the creature collapsing just feet from Jack's legs. The stampeding herd was like rolling thunder echoing throughout the valley.

Butch holstered his pistol and hefted Jack to his feet. "Are you all right?"

"I think so," he said, rubbing his shaky legs. "I'm not sure what happened."

Blood flowed from the buffalo's mangled eye as its front legs jerked and quivered.

Retrieving the rifle, Butch cranked its lever and fired into the creature's head. "Now do you see why the details are important?"

"I don't know what happened. I tried doing everything you said, but the rifle went off before I was ready."

"That's why you always leave your finger *outside* the trigger guard until you're ready for the shot." Butch cranked the lever again and collected the spent casings. "Keep your finger stretched out, pointing forward, until you're ready to squeeze. How many times have we gone over this?"

"I'm sorry, Butch."

"You two scared the wits outta me." Elijah came up behind them, placing a hand on Jack's shoulder. "You hurt?"

"I don't think so." He rubbed his shoulder. "Gonna be a tad sore for a few days, though."

"Here." Butch handed the rifle to Jack. "You and I are following the herd so we can finish this." Turning to Elijah, he gestured back toward the hillside. "Get someone to help you with cleaning this one, then follow after us for the others."

Jack held out the Winchester. "You better take this, I've caused enough problems."

"No sir." Butch pocketed the casings. "You're going to finish what you started."

Jack pushed the beans around his tin, waiting for the campfire ribbing to commence. Neither Butch nor Elijah, or any of the others for that matter, had so much as snickered or poked fun at him over the day's blunders.

"This may be the best buffalo I've ever gnawed on," Elijah said, cutting into another piece. "What you got on this, Henry?"

"Just salt."

"I don't normally take to buffalo"—Elijah gestured toward his plate—"but this here's mighty tasty."

"May be the best I've had as well," Butch said. "And we can all give thanks to Jack for felling this beast, feeding us all tonight."

The agreeing grunts and cheers didn't last long as the men refocused on their food.

Scanning faces for any smirks or giggles or sneaky grins, Jack shoveled another spoonful of beans into his mouth.

Henry cleared his throat in that way when you want everyone's attention. "I heard tell that Jim Leavy is about these parts."

Butch pushed his hat back on his head. "Jim Leavy? *Here?*"

"Is what I heard."

"What's that no-good sidewinder doing here?"

"Other than looking for a fight?" Henry shrugged. "I wouldn't have the foggiest."

"He'll find *exactly* what he's looking for if I run into him." Butch lit a cheroot and traipsed into the darkness. "I can promise you that much."

Jack waited a moment before leaning into Elijah. "Who's Jim Leavy?"

"Mostly a gambler and gunfighter. Gots a mean reputation as fast and efficient." He glanced into the darkness. "Gunned down Butch's cohort, Mike Casey, back in Nevada."

"You think he's here for Butch?"

"Hard to say." He sopped a biscuit in his beans. "But if Butch catches him out somewheres, it ain't gonna be pretty."

"I wouldn't know the man if I laid eyes on him."

"Oh you'd know Leavy if you happened upon *him*." Elijah's bewildered look soured. "One of Casey's friends shot the Irish bastard in the jaw, leaving him disfigured and downright grotesque."

"Think Butch could beat him to the draw?"

"I imagine it'd be close, for sure. But Leavy's got more of a reputation for calm accuracy than just fast-draw theatrics."

Soft harmonica notes emanated from somewhere about the campfire, intermingling a familiar, yet unidentifiable melody with the popping and cracking.

"How did Butch end up joining the gang?"

"He come to us, asked if we had room for another gun. Didn't take long at all to realize just how good he was."

"Was Pa the leader back then?"

"Sure enough." His smile widened. "But Jimmy was groomin' Butch almost from the very beginning."

"To take over as leader?"

Elijah went back to sopping. "To grow up and take responsibility for more than just his own self."

Jack rode next to Butch on horseback as they led the wagon into a mud-filled valley entrance. Shifting in his saddle, he spat an amber stream of tobacco. "This has to be the smallest town I've ever witnessed."

"Ain't a town," Butch said, surveying the surroundings. "It's a trading post."

"Well it's the smallest *trading post* I've ever seen."

The building was but a house made from crude logs and daubing. A covered porch gave shelter to the front door as well as a window to its right.

"Stay close when we get inside." Jabbing a thumb over his shoulder, Butch slowed the pace. "The others will unload everything while we negotiate."

A single horse stood hitched at the bottom of the sloped knoll where the building rested at the top. Rocks jutted from the muddy footpath leading to the entrance, encouraging hope of sure footing and dry clothing.

"Let me handle the conversations," Butch said, dismounting. "Your job is to watch my back. That is all."

"Got it."

Dank hides and burnt coffee lingered in the air just inside the main room, where an elderly woman smiled from a cluttered counter. "You boys like something to drink?" Her voice was shaky, thin.

"No thank you, ma'am." Butch made his way toward her. "But we sure do appreciate the hospitality."

"Looking for anything in particular?"

"Got a wagon full of buffalo hides." Butch motioned to the door. "Like to see about selling them."

Squinting, the woman leaned forward. "You boys don't look much like skinners."

"We thought we'd try our hands at hunting for the railroad." He rubbed the back of his neck. "While we're moving through the territory."

"Let me guess." A perceptive smile wrinkled her face. "You boys have *extra* pelts you're now aimin' to sell on the side."

Butch grinned. "Yes, ma'am. That about sums it up."

Jack studied the room, taking note of an open doorway, leading to another room to the right.

"These hides. They ain't gonna put me in a stinky predicament, are they?"

"No ma'am, these were not acquired while hunting on railroad time."

A single chuckle shook her chest and head. "That don't mean nothin' to the railroad folk."

"I can promise you, the men in our camp who felled these beasts are not even signed up by the railroad."

"I gotta hand it to you." Her smile widened. "You're pretty sharp for a dull fella."

A crashing came from the next room, sounding as though something had been knocked over or dropped.

Butch met Jack's gaze and nodded in the direction where the ruckus came from.

Removing the Colt from his belt, Jack crept through the doorway, scouring the room for movement.

Among the stacks of hides and blankets and cookware, the shelving was filled with every imaginable item a man would need on or off the trail.

"Sorry about the racket."

Jack jerked his aim toward the voice as a rush of adrenaline stabbed his nerves.

"W-whoa, whoa!" A tall figure emerged from the darkness of the far corner, hands raised. "Didn't mean to startle you."

Jack held his stance and aim. "What are you doing in here?"

"I was—"

"Everything all right?" Butch stood in the doorway with a hand on his sidearm.

"I was just trying to tell your friend here that I accidentally knocked over these shovels while reaching for that frying pan."

Butch moved his gaze from the man to the shovels and then to the shelf. "Put away your piece, Jack." He stepped closer to the man. "I apologize, we've been on the trail a bit too long."

"No need to apologize." The man took the skillet from the shelf and made his way to the main room. "The trail can make a fella right jumpy, it can."

After the stranger was gone, Butch placed a hand on Jack's shoulder. "I'm gonna go fetch one of the hides for the old woman to look over." He picked up a plug of tobacco and tossed it to Jack. "Gather all the items we discussed."

"Will do."

Jack carried several things to the counter where the woman was preoccupied with folding blankets.

"Where do you keep the cookin' flour?"

The woman finally looked up. "Your name Butch Carver?"

Jack squinted. "Why do you wanna know?"

Handing him a slip of paper, she shrugged. "Fella who just left told me to give that to you."

Jack glanced at the door, then back to the woman, who had already gone back to her folding. Opening the note, Jack made his way to the seclusion of the next room before Butch returned.

"I'm going to give you a fighting chance," the words read. "I will be waiting at the Palace Hotel. If, however, you choose to take the yellow trail, you will find my generosity sorely lacking."

Jack's stomach roiled at the sight of the signature. "Jim Leavy."

He's here for Butch. Jack read the note again, searching for anything he could find between the words. *He's come for Butch.*

"Everything all right?"

"Yeah." Jack tucked the note into a pocket as he turned to face Butch. "Just makin' sure I got everything."

CHAPTER 3

THE LATE-MORNING HEAT squeezed Jack's lungs, oppressing his *innards* as much as his *outtards,* as his Aunt Bessie used to say. And just like the sweltering Kentucky summers, the manure-laced breezes here did very little in the way of cooling anything in the torrid Wyoming pot.

"Gimme a hand, Jack." Henry tossed a rope across the wagon's buffalo hides. "Tighten that down and tie it off."

Feeding the braided hemp through a slat, Jack pulled it taut before working a simple knot. "Come see if this is up to snuff."

Henry tugged at the rope, nodded. "Hey, why don't you ride into town with me and help get these hides to the railroaders?"

The arid soil carried the scent of rain—yet not a hint of cloud could be found.

"Sure. Just let me visit the necessary first."

Finding a spot behind a decent bull pine, he gazed into the big blue sky where a Red-Tailed Hawk circled in silence and majesty. Jack shivered—either from the sight of the bird or from the relieving sensation of making water.

On his way back to the wagon, he clutched the slip of paper inside his pocket while fixing his gaze to Butch, who appeared to be cleaning his rifle on the far side of camp.

"Where you off to in such a trot?" Elijah seemed to step out from nowhere. "You let on like they handin' out sorghum cake in town or somethin'."

"Sweet Jesus, you scared the ever-lovin' bird turds outta me."

"I guess so, you was comin' through here like you was paintin' the camp with peyote."

Jack ran his thumb across the note still in his pocket. "I'm on my way to help Henry take the new hides into town."

"Then you best get to it." He slapped Jack on the back. "You sure don't want to keep that cantankerous buzzard waitin'."

Jack's gaze moved to the figure cleaning the rifle in the distance. "What do you think *he's* up to?" he said, jutting his chin toward Butch.

"If I was a bettin' man, I'd say he makin' preparations for Jim Leavy." Elijah smiled. "But I ain't no bettin' man . . . and I *still* say he makin' preparations for Leavy."

"Butch ain't gonna have to worry none about that feller."

Elijah turned back to him. "Now what on earth is *that* supposed to mean?"

Jack shrugged. "I just figure that Leavy feller don't really want no part of Butch Carver is all."

Another bluff of heat washed over them and was gone as quickly as it showed up.

"You best not be workin' up any preparations on your own, you hear?"

Jack let go of the note in his pocket and adjusted his hat. "I better get going. Like you said, I don't want Henry fussin' and sworpin' any more than usual."

Even though there wasn't much to speak of, the town bustled with activity. Wagons coming and going, men loading and unloading items of all sorts and sizes, and folks standing around waiting for something or someone or seemingly nothing in particular.

"Everyone keeps calling this place *town*," Jack said as they neared a mass of buildings. "Just plain ol' *town*. I don't reckon I've heard anybody use its name."

"Evanston. Named after some railroad official."

Jack leaned forward, pointing toward an enormous structure in the distance. "What in tarnation is *that*?"

"Roundhouse. It's where they work on engines and such."

"Is that where we're going?"

"No." He motioned toward a two-story building that seemed to be the center of business in town. "*That's* the Union Pacific office."

A distant clanging came from the direction of that immense edifice down the tracks—a metal to metal rhythmic dinging you'd normally hear from a blacksmith's shop.

"Seeing how the saloon is just next door, reckon we could have a few 'fore we head back to camp?" He grinned. "I mean, when we're done with business, of course."

"We'll see." Henry climbed down from the bench, stretched. "You stay with the hides while I go settle up with these high-benders."

The clanging continued in the distance, intermingled with an occasional steam whooshing.

Jack's stomach gurgled when he spotted the Palace Hotel just on the other side of the saloon. Long pull-down flags and pleated fan bunting gave the front of the establishment a very patriotic and official appearance.

"Newspaper?"

The boy standing beside the wagon couldn't have been more than ten or eleven, but something about the darkness around his eyes revealed life had aged him more than his years.

"What?"

"Newspaper." The boy held one up for Jack to see. "*Uinta County Herald*. Wanna buy one?"

"I ain't got no use for a blamed newspaper."

"Can't read?"

A familiar figure stepped out from the saloon's door. He wasn't carrying the pan he'd bought, but he was definitely the fellow from the trading post.

"I can read, you little bastard! Now go on and git!"

The man in front of the saloon turned his gaze toward Jack and instantly darted between the buildings.

"Hey!" Jack yelled as he leaped from the wagon. "Come back here!"

The man slipped into a doorway on the saloon side and disappeared into the darkness.

"I've got questions for you!" Jack put a hand on his Colt. "Stop acting like a coward and come face me!"

Stepping through the doorway, Jack scanned the space, which was obviously the saloon's storage area. Wooden crates lined the back wall, barely visible in the darkness. The ruckus from the main hall was muted, yet synonymous with nearly every saloon he'd ever frequented.

The stranger stood in the shadows at the far corner of the room. "Leave me be," he said without moving.

Jack raised his piece as he eased forward. "You're gonna tell me about that note you left at the tradin' post."

"I ain't got nothin' to say."

"You better have *plenty* to say." Jack inched closer, maintaining his aim on the silhouette. "You're ridin' with that Jim Leavy feller, ain't ya?"

The silhouette shifted without a reply.

"Answer me!"

Movement from the darkness at Jack's right caught his attention, just as pain exploded in his hand when something knocked the Colt from his grip.

A weathered boot quickly pinned the weapon to the floor as Jack scrambled to recover it.

"You're not Butch Carver." The voice made an odd slushing sound with each syllable. When the light from the door revealed the man's scars and misaligned jawline, Jack stepped back with a coldness in his gut.

"Jim Leavy." The name came out of Jack before he could stop it.

"Thatsh right."

Jack barely had time to blink when he caught a glimpse of the pistol butt barreling toward his face.

CHAPTER 4

THE DARKNESS SHIFTED with garbled and glugging sounds that reminded Jack of swimming the depths of Green River as a kid.

He forced his matted eyelids open and winced at the sunlight coming through what appeared to be ornate parlor windows of some luxury locomotive car.

Mahogany wainscoting, velveteen curtains, and opulent gas lamps stood out among the cabin's countless decorative features.

Attempting to sit up, Jack caught his balance when he realized he'd actually been standing the entire time.

What in blazes?

He quickly ran his hand over his nose and face but found no pain, no blood, not one thing out of the ordinary.

"There you are."

Turning, Jack found a refined gentleman seated on a leather burgundy sofa, combing his hair to the side.

His single-breasted morning jacket was brown ribbed worsted coating with the edges and cuffs bound with fine braid, a collarless waistcoat of white fancy quilting, and bright brown stripe trousers.

"Please . . ." He motioned toward a matching wingback chair. "Make yourself comfortable."

Jack held his gaze to the stranger's cold blue eyes while trying to put a finger on why his voice sounded familiar. "Where am I?"

"I have to admit." The man pocketed the comb and lit a rotund cigar. "I have searched the world high and low to locate you."

"What are you talking about?"

"I'd like to offer you a job, Mr. McCall—one that will make yours a household name for generations to come."

"How do you know my name?" Jack sat forward, scanning the quarters. "Are you with that Jim Leavy feller?"

THE DEADWOOD DEAL

Rising, the stranger made his way to a mirrored shelf and poured a glass of whiskey from a lavish decanter. "I'll get right to the point. There's a certain individual whom I wish to become . . . let's say . . . bereft of life."

There was something about the way the man spoke that was very much reminiscent of Doc McDowell—especially his accent and use of highfalutin words and phrases.

Jack got to his feet. "So you *are* with that lowdown murderer! Well you can get it outta your head right now, Mister . . ."

"I fear you misunderstand my intentions." Extending a hand, the man stepped closer. "For the sake of anonymity, why don't you just call me John Varnes."

Jack refused the handshake. "I'd just as soon die as to help you kill Butch Carver!"

"I assure you, Butch Carver is *not* my concern." He shrugged. "And neither is Jim Leavy, for that matter."

"I don't think I—"

"In exchange for your services, Mr. McCall, I'm willing to make you . . . bulletproof."

Jack cocked his head. "You some kind of politician or somethin'? Promisin' to keep the law outta my hair if I do as you ask?"

"I'm afraid not." Varnes poured another whiskey and handed it to Jack. "I mean precisely what I say—you will *physically* become bulletproof."

Pain exploded throughout Jack's face as he awakened on a saloon table, stretched out on his back, with a cluster of men standing over him.

"He's coming to!" The booming voice startled Jack into sitting up.

"Easy there," an older man soothed while gentle hands moved his shoulders back to the table. "You've been out for a while. You had us worried."

Squinting from the painful light, Jack reached for his face, searching for the source of agony.

A hand caught his wrist and moved his arm back to his side. "Take it easy, son, your nose is busted up pretty bad and both your eyes are turning purple."

"Where'd he go?"

"Who?" The man pulled one of Jack's bottom eyelids down and leaned closer. "Barkeep found you in the back looking like you'd been kicked in the face by a bank mule. Found your Colt a few feet away."

"The fella from the train." Jack's own voice brought misery to his head. "Where'd he go?"

"Just settle down." The man checked Jack's other eye. "I'm Doc Zornes. I'm gonna give you some laudanum for the pain."

"I don't need no laudanum." Jack moved to sit up again, and again allowed the hands to ease him back to the table.

"Son, you're gonna need all you can get your hands on when I start working on resetting that snout of yours."

Scrunching his nose, Jack immediately winced as another stab of pain came as quickly as the welling tears. "Shit!"

Zornes chuckled. "Do you see what I mean? That's why I'm giving you the—"

"Listen to me!" Jack groped at the man's lapels. "There was a fella here just a few minutes ago . . . well, not *here* . . . he was inside some fancy railcar."

"You took a terrible blow to the head, son. You're probably seeing things that aren't really there. It's a common thing with head trauma like yours."

"I know what I saw!"

Pulling away, the doctor motioned toward the doors. "You mean that fella with the wagon of buffalo hides Leavy took after?"

"What?" Jack pushed hands away as he sat up. "I need a horse!"

"Son, you're in no shape to—"

"Listen to me!" Jack moved to his feet, stuffing the Colt into the waistband of his trousers. "I need a horse *now*!"

Whistling wind carried dirt and debris through camp as Jack tied the mare he'd appropriated from the front of the saloon in town.

Scanning the area for activity, he noticed a few men standing over something. "Hey, did Henry come back this way?"

The individuals turned to Jack and steadily parted when he made his way toward them, revealing a figure on the ground at their feet.

"Henry?" Jack pushed past the men, dropped to his knees, and pulled the bloodied figure toward him. "Henry!"

Someone tugged at his arm. "He's dead, Jack."

"No . . ."

The men pulled him to his feet. "Come on, Jack. We've got to get outta here before that maniac returns."

Jack straightened. "Leavy?" He studied each man's face. "Did Leavy do this?"

One of the fellas shrugged. "It was some guy with a mangled-up face."

"Where's Butch?"

"Him and Elijah took after the fella."

"Which way did they go?"

"Don't know what's going on, Jack, but that man was here intentionally for Butch."

Jack focused on the man's face for the first time. "What are you talking about, Burgess?"

"It was like that fella knew Henry'd lead him straight to Butch." He shrugged. "It's bound to be the reason he chased him."

"Why would you say that?"

"After he killed Henry, he rode through camp yelling Butch's name." Burgess dropped his gaze to the ground. "He tore outta here when Elijah and the rest of us started sending lead in his direction."

"He was ridin' through so fast, I don't reckon nary a bullet found a lick of flesh," one of the other men added.

Burgess cocked his head. "Next thing I know'd, Butch and Elijah tore outta here on horseback, yelling for us to stay with Henry."

Jack waited a moment, moving his gaze from one man to the next. "Well?"

Burgess stood motionless, maintaining a baffled expression.

Lifting his arms with an exaggerated shrug, Jack shook his head. "Which way did they go?"

Jack followed the trail of stirring dust as he scoured the valley for anything that could point him in the right direction.

Leavy must have knew Henry and Butch rode together.

The cumbrous sun weighed around his shoulders and neck—an albatross soaking his grubby collar with perspiration.

Reaching for the anguish in his face again, Jack winced as the searing stabs thrummed with every heartbeat, the wind against his face forcing tears toward his earlobes.

Why else would he go after Henry?

Gunshots rang out from a short distance ahead, instantly halting the gelding, the poor critter bobbing its head in protest.

"Let's go!" Jack yelled, striking the reins.

The agony in his head grew with every movement of the ride, seemingly as though something was expanding inside his skull.

The trail eventually opened into a fog of thick dust settling in every direction.

Slowing to listen closer, Jack turned in the saddle when a breeze rustled through twisted, shabby trees, carrying a hint of cigar smoke.

"We have some unfinished business, don't you think?"

Jack fumbled for his piece as an icy stab ran the length of his spine. The coldness swelled when he found John Varnes sitting cross legged on a wingback chair in the middle of the wilderness, a smoldering cigar just inches from his face.

"Shit!" Jack took aim. "How did you—"

"We don't have a lot of time . . . especially with what you're about to encounter."

Jack searched the surroundings for a horse or wagon or anything that could make sense of any of this. "You some kinda haint?"

Smiling, Varnes drew on the cigar. "I'm afraid you are about to embark on a situation where my offer would be quite advantageous," he said, exhaling smoke.

Jack tried to steady his aim. "What do you mean?"

"Very shortly, in just mere minutes, you are going to find yourself in a situation where the benefits of our agreement could mean life or death for you." He rose to his feet. "And you are of no use to me dead."

"Where is Butch and Elijah? Did they come through this way?"

Retrieving an envelope from his jacket's inside pocket, Varnes stepped forward. "All you have to do is take care of my problem, and your issue will no longer be an issue."

"Look, I ain't no murderer. I don't know what gave you that

idea. I don't even know who you are . . . or *what* you are for that matter."

Varnes removed the folded paper from the envelope and held it out. "You don't have to pretend with me."

Jack took the document, looked over the fancy handwriting. "There's not even a name listed for the feller you want—"

"You'll know him when you meet him." Varnes smiled. "You won't have to worry about that."

Jack studied the man's eyes. "What if I say no?"

"I'll just find someone else." Shrugging, Varnes held out a writing instrument. "Possibly sooner than it will take for anyone to find your rotting corpse out here."

"You threatenin' me?"

The quietude on the trail brought a sourness to Jack's stomach as he rode further into the openness.

He poked at his chest with an index finger, examining the pressure and tenderness of fingernail against flesh.

What am I doing? He wiped his finger down his jacket and refocused on the surroundings. *Varnes is a lunatic.*

A darkened spot in the distance stood out from the landscape's dust, rocks, and vegetation.

Holding his gaze on the motionless shape, Jack urged the horse along with caution.

He massaged his forehead, hoping to relieve the misery. "Shoulda asked to be *painproof* instead of bulletproof."

Jack drew his piece, directing it toward a silhouette when he caught a glimpse of movement.

"You best turn back if ya know what's good for you," a strained voice said from the bleeding man on the ground.

"Elijah?" Jack dismounted and dropped next to him. "Are you ok?"

Elijah stared off to the right. "Is that you, Jack?" He put a trembling hand on his chest and coughed. "You needs to git on outta here."

Jack leaned closer. "Where's Butch?"

"Don't you worry none about Butch. Butch can care for his own self." He coughed again, sending specks of crimson onto his cheeks and chin. "Git on that horse and head back the way you came."

"You know I can't—"

"You should lishen to your friend."

Coldness bloomed in Jack's legs and torso as he turned toward Jim Leavy. The man's stance was a confident lean with a palm resting on his sidearm.

Jack couldn't tell if Leavy was offering a smirk of a grin, or if the scars just twisted up his mouth that way. "Go to hell."

"Thatsh just downright rude, boy." There was no doubt it was a smile now twisting into place. "I'd exshpect a bit more gratitude from someone I left with little more than a busted nose."

"Where's Butch?"

Leavy squinched his eyes. "Amid the flames o' hell by now, I'd wager."

"You . . . " Jack turned his piece toward the Irishman and began firing.

Reports from Leavy's gun intermingled with Jack's as the two men moved for cover.

Jack's legs weakened and his chest tightened as he searched for a safe spot to retreat.

The horse Jack brought fidgeted at the ruckus before buckling swiftly to the ground.

Gun smoke lingered in the air with the faintest of a breeze.

Trying to keep his gaze to Leavy, Jack tripped over a rock and came down hard on his side. The pain in his ribs seemed connected directly to his throbbing face.

He examined his side with a trembling hand but found no blood, no bullet wounds.

Upon realizing the shooting had ended, Jack noticed Leavy was no longer in the place he'd been firing from.

"You all right, Elijah?"

The sounds of a galloping horse echoed as Leavy came into view as he rode back toward town.

Turning to Elijah, Jack noticed the fresh bullet hole in his friend's forehead. "Elijah?"

CHAPTER 5

THE CAMPFIRE CRACKLED and popped as the night air washed over the handful of men gathered at what was left of their camp.

"What are we to do now, Jack?" The dirt stains on Burgess's undershirt were a mournful reminder of the three men they'd buried just hours earlier.

"I ain't got no clue." Jack stared blankly ahead. "Why are you askin' me?"

"I reckon it's the thing to talk over." Burgess spit tobacco toward the fire. "Should we head out in the morning or stay put for a day or so?"

One of the other men leaned forward. "Word in town is Leavy has already packed and gone."

Jack lifted his chin. "What direction they sayin' he took?"

"Nobody's made that clear."

"Just so you know, I'm leavin' first thing in the mornin'." Jack focused on the fire. "I'm headin' out on my own."

"You oughta stay with us for a few days longer," Burgess said. "We can all use some time to think before we start making decisions."

"I ain't stayin' here any longer than I have to."

"I understand." There was resignation in Burgess's voice. "You've been through quite a bit today. And Lady Luck seemed to have been by your side the whole time."

Jack gently touched his aching nose. "If Lady Luck was with me, I'd sure hate to think of what my day woulda been without her."

"Elijah got a bullet smack-dab twixt his eyes." Burgess shook his head. "That horse you road out there on took a bullet to the side of the head and was probably dead 'fore it hit the ground." He shrugged. "You survived without a slug one, and *you* were the one Leavy was shooting at."

"Yeah, well maybe he's just not as good as they let on."

"You know better than that. That fella shot Henry from a distance while riding through camp." Burgess forced air from his lips. "We all know how good Butch was, right? And you saw what the man did to Butch . . . no sir, Lady Luck was practically holding your hand."

Jack stared deeper into the fire. "Y'all ever heard of John Varnes?"

One of the men took a swig from a bottle and handed it to Jack. "Who?"

Jack wiped the top with a shirtsleeve before taking a drink. "John Varnes." He handed the whiskey to Burgess. "I met him in one of them fancy rail cars."

"I don't recall anyone named Varnes," Burgess said with a shrug. "Is he from around these parts?"

Jack reached for the whiskey again. "I'm fairly certain Varnes ain't from around here."

The front of the trading post appeared abandoned when Jack pulled the wagon to the hitching rail with his horse ponied.

He shifted his Colt in his waistband as he headed toward the open door where the old woman stood staring out at him.

"Can't be good news when you come traipsin' in here all by your lonesome."

Jack removed his hat, wiped a gritty sleeve across his forehead. "You'd be correct in that assumption, ma'am."

Stepping out on the porch, the woman shielded her eyes from the sunlight. "You wouldn't be bringin' trouble with you, now would you?"

"At this point, I don't rightly know what to expect."

"You look like you could use a bit of bourbon." She turned to go inside. "I can already tell I'm gonna need some myself."

There was a sweet smell just inside, but not in a pleasant manner.

"You looking to sell those hides?"

Placing his hat back on his head, Jack nodded. "Looking to sell the whole rig . . . except for my horse."

She put a half-empty bottle on the counter and stared into Jack. "I got myself a bad feeling about this."

Jack uncorked the bourbon, took a drink, and slid the bottle back across the counter. "Tell you what, you let me collect a few supplies and I'll just leave the rig and hides."

She took a drink. "I fear the trouble it's bound to bring me."

"What's a proprietor to do when someone just abandons things right outside their door?"

A grin eventually stretched across her face. "You got ten minutes . . . and I better never see you around here again."

On his way back toward the wagon, Jack noticed a tethered horse that hadn't been there when he'd gone inside. He scanned the landscape without moving his head, just as Butch had taught him.

Keeping his Colt at the ready, Jack secured the supplies to his horse, mounted up, and eased back to the trail.

The mysterious critter wasn't Leavy's, nor was it the horse of the fella running with the Irishman as best Jack could recollect. *I woulda surely heard if someone had entered the building while I was gathering items.*

He kept glancing over his shoulder as his horse trotted along without any sign of alarm or caution.

Where the hell am I goin'? He yanked at the collar that kept riding up his neck. *And which direction would Leavy be heading?*

It only took a few hours in the saddle before Jack was rubbing at his backside. After a bit of numbness and soreness, he found a clearing and secured the horse.

Stretching, he gazed over the area before finding a spot to relieve himself. Darkness would be upon him soon so he decided to set up camp for the night.

Once he had a fire started, he took a few pieces of jerked beef from his pack and nibbled. He'd been riding west, but not intentionally or with a specific destination in mind.

The fire's warmth permeated his clothing, rebuking the night air, soothing his nose and face.

A warbling groan came from the horse as it shifted.

Turning to check on the beast, Jack recoiled at the sudden cold metal against his temple.

"Keep your hands right where they are." It was a soft, growl-of-a-voice from behind. "Hand me that piece you've got tucked at your side. I don't wanna kill you, but I will if you force me to."

The man's voice wasn't familiar, but Jack strained to attach it to someone he may have encountered in the past. "Who are you with?"

"Just keep your mouth shut and do as I say."

The stench from the stranger reminded Jack of his days working with the hogs back at his grandfather's farm.

"Give me the money and I'll leave you with your horse and supplies."

Jack dug into a pocket and retrieved a small leather pouch. Holding it out, he noticed the wrinkling in the stranger's hands and face. "You gonna leave my piece as well?"

"Shut up." The man opened the pouch's mouth and emptied the contents into a filthy palm. "What's this?"

Jack moved his gaze from the coins to the man's face. "What do you mean?"

"What do I mean?" His frown turned to clenched teeth. "Where's the money?"

"I don't think I follow what you mean." He nodded toward the coins. "You've got the money right there."

The man balled his fist around the silver pieces. "Drop the simpleton routine, boy!" He stepped closer, keeping the muzzle against Jack's head. "I followed you from the trading post after you sold them hides and wagon. So where's the money?"

Heat spread into the back of Jack's neck. "I didn't sell anything. And if that old hag said I did, then she lied to you."

"I'm going to give you one last chance." The words came through still-clenched teeth. "If you don't tell me where the money is, I'll spread your brains across this fire and search for it myself."

"Look, I'll empty my pockets, strip down naked if you want . . . and even unpack everything from the horse." Jack shrugged. "But what little bit you got in your hand is all the money there is."

The man's eyebrows came down together. "Just shut your yappin'." He stuffed the bits into a pocket and shook his head. "I can't believe I followed you all this way for little more than a handful of nickels."

A branch shifted in the fire, sending a light burst of embers into the air.

"And I can't just let you go now, can I?"

The warmth drained from Jack's neck and chest. "Listen—"

"I said shut up!" He added pressure to the muzzle against Jack's temple. "I need to think."

Jack closed his eyes and tried to slow his breathing.

"I'm sorry, fella." The man ratcheted the hammer back. "But I can't take any chances."

Jack braced himself, squeezing his eyes shut. But the firearm offered nothing more than an empty click.

Without hesitation, Jack knocked the gun from his head and wrestled the thief to the ground.

The man wasn't as large as he'd appeared to be when he was standing over Jack. And now on the ground, he seemed nothing more than a scrawny old timer.

Clenching the fella's throat with one hand, Jack struggled to regain control of his own pistol. "You ain't so tough now, are ya?"

The old man abruptly clutched at Jack's grip with both hands, giving up the Colt in the struggle. His gasping turned to coughing, his coughing to dry heaves.

Putting the muzzle of his piece to the man's forehead, Jack grimaced. "Are you alone?"

The man's face reddened from his struggles. "Please don't kill me."

"Answer the question."

"I swear I'll ride in any direction you tell me to go. Just don't kill me." He held his hands up in surrender. "I have young'uns to feed."

"I'm afraid your young'uns are fixin' to starve."

Blood spattered Jack's arms and face when the gun went off.

He sat quietly until the ringing in his ears subsided before retrieving his money. "Those kid's oughta be old enough to fend for themselves by now anyway."

CHAPTER 6

THE **SALOON TABLE** looked as though it may have been used for shelter during some horrific battle. Deep scarring marred the wood, along with cigar-shaped burns at its edges.

Shoveling another spoonful of stew into his mouth, Jack kept tabs on the activity taking place between his seat in the far corner and the door.

The beef was tough and damn near tasteless, but as long as customers kept buying whisky, the grub was complimentary.

Four men occupied a nearby gambling table, each focusing so intently on the hands they'd been dealt, anyone who wasn't familiar with the game would probably think they were ignoring one another.

"If you'd spend a little more time shuffling the deck instead of running your mouth, we wouldn't keep playin' the same hands over and over," one of the men finally said, tossing his cards to the center of the table.

Grumbles and murmuring followed as the others surrendered their hands to the pot.

The ride had been a long and arduous one, especially with the efforts of being more vigilant along the way.

Leavy could be anywhere by now.

Cold air washed over the room when a husky fella came through the door sporting a clean shirt and britches that didn't quite match his stature.

A Colt hung high on his hip, cavalry-draw style, with the flap clearly cut from the holster.

Smiling at the bartender, the man ambled toward the bar, revealing another figure who'd followed in behind him.

The fancy attire of the second individual stood out among the common folk, yet no one seemed to pay him any mind as he made his way toward Jack's table.

THE DEADWOOD DEAL

"I'm glad to see you are traveling in the correct direction," John Varnes said, taking a seat.

"I ain't got no clue as to what you're up to." Jack tapped an index finger to his temple. "But there ain't a doubt in my mind, you're tetched in the head."

"In spite of last night's altercation, you still don't believe yourself to be bulletproof?"

"For one thing, the thief's pistol jammed when . . . " He paused a moment. "How did you know about last night?"

"Do you play?" The man lit a cigar.

Jack noticed the bartender studying him as he turned back to Varnes. "What the hell is that supposed to mean?"

"Poker." He gestured toward the men still playing. "Do you know how to play?"

"Of course. I'm more familiar with Faro, but I've taken part in about every gambling game you can imagine."

"Good. It will come in handy when you get to Deadwood."

"Deadwood? Dakota Territory?"

"That's right." Varnes fiddled with one of his cufflinks. "The gentleman I have contracted you to . . . deal with . . . will be there." He drew on his cigar. "I use the term *gentleman* very loosely here, mind you."

"Who are you really?"

Varnes leaned back in his chair. "Why, Mr. McCall, I've already explained that you may call me John Varnes."

"I got that. But you know damn well that ain't what I'm gettin' at."

It took a moment before Varnes smiled. "I know you are interested in more details, Mr. McCall." Leaning forward, he fixed his gaze to Jack's. "But for anonymity purposes, *John Varnes* will have to suffice."

"The only thing I'm interested in right now is finding Jim Leavy."

"I'm afraid vengeance will not satiate the hunger you now carry, my boy."

Jack raised his eyebrows. "Says the man that's hired me to kill some feller in order to satisfy his own vengeance."

"Ah, but *that* is where you are incorrect. I am but a mere debt collector. Vengeance is not mine, emotions do not rule my motives." He flicked ashes to the floor. "And you, my good man, are simply collecting a debt on my behalf."

"Call it what you will, but it's all the same if you ask me."

"Tell me something." Varnes put his elbows on the table and leaned in. "Why are you so hell bent on Jim Leavy?"

Jack searched the man's eyes. "You're joking, right?" He stole a glance at the door before turning back. "He killed Butch, killed Elijah, and killed Henry!"

"Let's be rational. How do you know he was the one who committed all those atrocities?"

"Waddaya mean *how do I know*? I was there."

Varnes drew on his cigar, leaned back in the chair. "Well, to be fair, you only *heard* that Leavy killed Henry." He stared at the butt of his cigar. "Sure, Elijah died during a gun battle between you and Leavy, but you can't be certain it wasn't a ricocheting bullet of his or yours that did him in. And there are absolutely no witnesses to the death of Butch Carver."

"Leavy was the only other person out there!"

Varnes tilted his head. "Can you be certain of that?"

"Leavy even said—"

"Jim Leavy speculated that Butch was *amid the flames of hell* when you asked where he was." He brought the cigar closer to his lips. "A far cry from admission to murder, I would think."

Jack started to stand but leaned closer. "What are you gettin' at?"

Varnes shrugged. "What if it was someone else?"

"Do you know something you ain't tellin'?"

"I don't know, do I . . . Jack?"

"What the hell is *that* supposed to mean?"

Varnes drew again from the cigar. "You've talked quite a bit about Jim Leavy, but you haven't said one word about what you found when you discovered Butch."

Jack picked up his whiskey and immediately put it back on the table. "I don't want to talk about it."

"Oh, I think you *want* to talk about it." His gentle tone did little to soften the lingering chill in his eyes. "And I understand your worries of being overcome with emotion."

Jack tried to swallow the tightness that crept into his throat.

"After all, this is one of your closest friends we're talking about." Varnes barely nodded. "More than likely, you regarded Butch Carver far more closely than you did your very own family. Why, I would even go so far as to say you probably thought of him as a brother."

THE DEADWOOD DEAL

The saloon's quietude produced a ringing in Jack's head, very similar to what is experienced after one fires a scattergun.

Cigar smoke stung Jack's eyes as the tightening in his throat became a lump of dryness. "He looked to be sleepin' on a small plateau of rocks." Trying to swallow again, Jack closed his eyes. "Just as peaceful as could be."

"Tell me what you saw."

Rubbing a knuckle over an eyebrow, Jack shook his head. "I just remember there was so much blood." The ringing seemingly grew. "Front of his shirt was soaked with it."

"Was there anything that seemed . . . *odd* to you?"

"There was no blood on his face. I remember that vividly for some reason."

"What about his hands?" Varnes blew smoke toward the ceiling. "Did you notice anything strange about his hands?"

Jack flinched at the returning images. "No blood either."

"Did you notice what he was *holding*?"

Jack shrugged. "He wasn't holding anything."

Dipping his chin toward his chest, Varnes lifted his brows for effect. "Nothing at all?"

"Nothing. He just looked as though . . ." Jack rubbed his aching forehead. "His pistols were still in their holsters."

"It sounds as though someone else could have took him by surprise."

Jack caught another glimpse of the gawking bartender. "Is there anything I can help you with?" he called across the room.

The proprietor turned away as though embarrassed, straightening bottles on the backbar as he moved.

"I've gotta watch my back now closer than ever before."

"After everything thus far," Varnes said, shaking his head. "You still do not believe yourself to be bulletproof?"

"I'll be honest with you, at this point, I don't believe much."

Varnes got to his feet. "Well then," he said, picking up his chair. "Let's make you a believer, shall we?"

In one fluid motion, he raised the chair over and behind his head and hurled it toward the bar where it crashed against the big man standing there.

Jack rose, watching as the crimson-faced fella turned toward him and Varnes.

Except Varnes was no longer there.

"If you're looking for trouble, boy, you've sure found it." The man shoved an empty table out of the way as he approached.

"Now hold on." Jack held up his hands. "There's been a misunderstanding."

"You better believe there's been a misunderstanding," he said, yanking Jack by the lapels. "A very *big* misunderstanding."

Scrambling for his piece, Jack barely had time to wince before the ham-of-a-fist slammed into his face, intensifying the pain that was already there.

Had the man not been holding him with that other ham, Jack would have been sprawled out on the floor, counting ceiling beams.

"So help me, if you manage to get that pistol outta your belt, you're gonna have an even bigger misunderstanding on your hands." The man's Colt was now directed at Jack's head as he finally released him.

"I didn't—"

"Shut your mouth!" he said, motioning his revolver toward Jack's. "Just hand over the Peacemaker before you start taking heed to any other unhealthy ideas."

"If you'll just listen, I can—"

The man pulled back the hammer. "This is your last chance, boy."

Sourness crept from Jack's stomach into his chest and throat. "All right. All right." He carefully pulled the Colt from his belt, holding it close.

"Hand it over."

The sourness festered in Jack's throat. "I tell you what," he said, bringing the piece up, aiming it at the man's head. "Why don't you come and get it."

That intensive stare never wavered, it was as though the big fella hadn't heard Jack's words, hadn't noticed the Colt's bead on him. But then his left eye twitched.

At first, Jack believed his was the only report when he fired, but the sting in his shoulder, and smoke wafting from the man's piece, told a different story.

With blank eyes fixed on something unseen, the big fella groped at the widening bloodstain on his chest before dropping to the floor like a felled oak.

A warm breeze circulated the room as a few patrons scrambled out the door.

"Hells bells," the bartender said, moving closer. "You killed Virgil."

"He tried to kill *me*! You saw the whole thing." Jack returned the Colt to his belt. "He even got me in my shoulder." He reached for the wound and brought back a dry hand.

"You don't look hit." The bartender stepped closer to inspect. "What's your name?"

"Jack McCall." Jack closed his eyes almost immediately, shaking his head. "I mean—"

"You got a few holes in your shirt, but nary a bloodstain." The man turned to the remaining patrons. "Somebody go and fetch the sheriff."

Sure enough there were two holes, but no pain, no blood, and no explanation. The fact that the two holes were so closely situated they could easily be mistaken for one long one did little to ease Jack's mind. "You seen where I tried to keep from fightin' that feller."

"Everybody knows Virgil's got a temper, and when you hit him with that chair . . . why you're lucky to be alive. He just don't miss like he did with you."

"I didn't throw that chair. It was that fancy feller that came back to the table. John Varnes. That's his name, John Varnes."

The barkeep's eyebrows came together. "Look, kid, I'm not trying to put the blame on you. I'm just saying you're one lucky man to be alive right now."

The gamblers were back to their card game as though nothing had happened.

"I best go fetch the sheriff myself." The bartender tossed a rag bchind the counter and made his way toward the door. "Hopefully he's not too drunk to come by."

Jack touched his shoulder again before downing what whiskey remained in his glass. *Shit.*

The gamblers didn't bother looking up from their cards as he quickly made his way to the door and his horse.

CHAPTER 7

WHEN FIRST COMING up to the tail end of a wagon train, Jack slowed his pace while focusing on getting a head count.

Looked to be just a few wagons with several flanking riders, but Jack made the effort to ride in the open, at a respectable distance. The last thing he wanted was to startle them with an unexpected approach.

It didn't take long before two riders split from the caravan and headed toward him in a reserved gallop.

The one leading the way had a dark brown beard with graying tufts at the chin, while the other looked to be too young to even shave.

"Didn't mean to startle you fellers," Jack called out before the two made it all the way to his position. "I wasn't expectin' to encounter anyone else out here."

"I reckon you're heading to Deadwood as well?" the older man asked, pushing his hat back on his head.

"That's the plan."

The man looked over Jack and his horse. "Ain't safe to be ridin' alone out here." He leaned over to his right and spat. "You runnin' from somebody or somethin'?"

A bead of sweat trickled Jack's backside. "Just got some business to tend, is all."

"I'm Luther Jackson." The man nodded toward his companion. "This here's my son, Clarence."

With the briefest of a nod, the younger fella moved his gaze anywhere he could to seemingly avoid Jack's.

"Nice to meet you fellers."

"I'm sure you understand our cautious nature. We can ill afford nary a chance on the trail."

Jack nodded. "I understand more than you know. But if you let me pass 'round you folks, you won't have to burden yourselves with maintaining an eye on a tailing stranger."

Luther daubed at his neck with a dingy bandana. "When's the last time you had a proper meal?"

"Other than jerked beef and hardtack? It's been a while."

The man nodded as though he knew the answer before Jack replied. "We're gonna set up camp here shortly. Why don't you let us get something in your belly before you move on?"

"I ain't lookin' to impose myself on y'all. But I sure do appreciate the gesture."

"You're *invited* . . . ain't the same as imposin'." He smiled. "Besides, I'd feel a whole heap better knowing we sent you ahead fully sustained."

"Suit yourself. I ain't about to turn down a hot meal."

"I think I should warn you, though." Luther pulled the reins to turn toward the wagons. "We have an old woman who'll want to speak with you at some point before you head out."

"Why is that a warning?"

Pulling the hat back where it belonged, Luther lifted his brows. "Let's just say Gran Mary's a different breed of cat altogether. That's all."

The woman plopped another slab of thick-cut bacon onto Jack's tin. "I'm going to bundle up some of these vittles for you to take with you on the trail."

"Thank you, ma'am." He tore off a hunk of bread. "If you don't mind me sayin' so, you sure don't look old enough to be called Gran Mary."

Putting a hand on her hip, the woman stared into him. "That's because I'm *not* Gran Mary."

"Oh . . . my apologies."

"None necessary." She pointed toward a sun-leathered woman sitting just behind the back end of one of the prairie schooners. "*That's* Gran Mary."

"It's my fault." Luther wiped his mouth with a shirtsleeve. "I shoulda introduced you to everyone already. This here's my wife, Betsy."

"Nice to meet you, ma'am."

Luther turned to Jack with a narrowing gaze. "Come to think of it, I don't recollect you ever giving your name."

"I didn't?" Jack rubbed his neck. "I'm Bill Sutherland."

"Well . . . you've already met—"

"Bring the stranger to me." The raspy voice came from the direction of Gran Mary.

The couple glanced at each other before Luther turned to Jack. "Don't say I didn't warn you."

"Warn me about what?"

"Stop it, Luther." Betsy gently slapped his arm before turning to Jack. "Gran Mary is just a bit odd is all. Luther and the boys let on like she's some kind of witch or something."

"She's really harmless," Luther said with a nod. "But you'll see what I'm talking about."

Gran Mary was threading a sewing needle when Luther led Jack to the wooden crate where the old woman sat. Her dress came all the way down to her feet and seemed to be made from old feed sacks.

"Here he is," Luther said with elevated volume. "His name is Bill Sutherland."

Gran Mary didn't look up as she matched the ends of her thread before tying a knot. "He'll be just dandy without you, Luther. Go on about your business."

Luther glanced at Jack. "Yes, ma'am."

An open jar sat on the back of the wagon near the old woman, its varied contents glinting in the setting sun. Next to the jar was a tin of colored threads and cloth patches.

"You from Wyoming?" She maintained her focus on her busy hands.

Jack eased onto a nearby crate. "Kentucky."

"Hmm." She pushed the needle into a thick fabric and pulled the thread through. "What did Luther say your name was?"

"Sutherland. Bill Sutherland."

She met Jack's gaze but kept working the needle. "Hmm."

Warmth gathered in Jack's cheeks, spreading to his ears and neck. The old woman's stare was like an imminent branding iron.

Clearing his throat, Jack gestured toward the back of the wagon. "What's in the canning glass?"

Gran Mary followed his gaze. "Oh . . . that's my crow jar."

Jack waited a moment for an explanation, then cleared his throat again when none came. "I don't reckon I've ever heard of a crow jar."

"A while back I started feeding the starving things when they came near." She tied a knot in the thread and trimmed it with a knife. "And before long a few of the crows brought back gifts to say thank you."

Jack leaned forward. "Gifts?"

"Uh huh." She retrieved the jar and poured a few of its contents into a wrinkled palm. "Shiny trinkets of metal, small slivers of painted wood, bone pieces, and beads."

"And they bring these things to you because you feed them?"

Her smile carried a glint of pride. "The kindness we show others will *always* develop into friendships and treasure."

Cocking his head, Jack squinted. "Are you sayin' they actually *put* the items in the jar?"

"Oh, no," she said with a laugh. "No, they leave the things in the same area I feed them so I can gather them up myself."

"I ain't never heard tell of anything like that." He shook his head. "I reckon this all took place before you folks started on the trail."

"That's where it *started*," she said, dumping the items back into the jar. "See that one getting closer? That's Maxwell. He was just a little thing when I first started feeding them."

"What? So the crows you're feeding on this here trail are the same crows you fed at home?"

"Oh yes." Her smile widened. "We reap that which we sow, you know. Sowing kindness will ensure kindness in return. And it will follow you for the rest of your days." Her smile faded. "But if we sow pain or hate or evil . . . " Her branding-iron gaze returned. "Then we can expect our remaining days to be a harvest of the same."

The warmth spread to Jack's chest and stomach. "Sounds like Sunday preachin' if you ask me."

"What happened to make your nose all crooked like that?"

Jack reached for his face but stopped short. "Feller hit me with a pistol."

"Hmm." She swirled the jar's items with a few fingers. "Just be mindful, evil almost always enters through our pain."

"Well." Jack slapped his knees and rose to his feet. "I best be headin' on out." He tipped his hat. "But I sure do appreciate the hospitality."

"Before you traipse off, I want to give you something." Retrieving several beads from the jar, she began stringing them onto a long piece of thread. "These are ghost beads."

"I feel like you're puttin' me on."

She added a few more without looking up. "They're made from dried juniper berries. The Navajo say these bring about peace, harmony, and safety."

Jack forced a smile. "What makes you think I need them?"

She tied the ends of the thread and cut the excess. "Because they're said to ward off evil spirits, ghosts, and nightmares."

"How do you . . . ?"

Handing the beads to him, she offered a resolute expression. "You don't have to wear them, but be sure and keep them with you at all times."

A flurry of wind washed over them with stinging grains of sand and debris.

"Have you ever heard of . . . " Jack shook his head.

The old woman studied his face a moment. "Have I ever heard of *what*?"

Jack tried to keep his focus away from the jar. "Oh, nothin'. I don't mean to keep you from your stitchin'."

She placed a smooth, cold hand on Jack's forearm. "You don't have to follow the shadow." She squeezed his arm gently. "Let the shadow follow behind *you* . . . Where it belongs."

The breeze picked up again as Jack searched her eyes. "What's that supposed to mean?"

Gran Mary went back to her sewing. "Look at the sun. Tell me what it's doing."

"Uh . . . " Jack searched the sky. "Setting?"

"Correct. And the exact same sun that is *setting* for you right now is, without a doubt, *rising* for someone else at this very moment." She smiled. "What's the difference?"

Jack shrugged.

She squeezed his arm. "It's where you stand, and when."

Jack considered her a moment before stashing the beads into a pocket. "Once again, thank you for the hospitality, ma'am."

CHAPTER 8

EADWOOD'S MUD-ENCRUSTED STREETS bustled with activity amid the mining supplies and saloons on seemingly every corner.

Jack breathed in the late July heat and winced at the heaviness in his lungs.

"Let's get you some water," he said, patting the horse's neck. "To be honest, I could use a drink or two myself."

A couple of young men lounged atop a small pile of lumber just next to a shabby tent with several shovels and tools set out for display.

"I can help you find the cheapest livery in town, mister." The young man scooted toward the edge of the lumber. "And they take real good care of the critters."

"Cheapest, huh?" Jack rubbed the stubble on his chin. "How much of a cut are they givin' you?"

"My uncle owns the place. I get a bed and regular meals." He shrugged. "That's about it."

The boy's oversized boots possessed far more years of wear than the young fella could possibly account for.

"Lead the way," Jack said.

Moving through the streets like a raccoon searching for food, the young man paused every few moments to make sure Jack was still following.

The thing that stood out more than anything was Deadwood's pace. It seemed as though everyone was in a rush. At least when compared to other towns and hollows.

No leisure strolls. No gallivanting about. No time to take in the stench from the strewn oddments and food scraps.

The livery was a bit larger than expected with rough-wood stalls lining the interior along with rough-cut saddle stands and piles of hay.

"Told you it was the best in town." The boy took Jack's horse by the reins and waited for him to climb down. "My uncle can also re-shoe if'n the need arises."

"What's the cost per week?"

Gesturing toward a handwritten list on the wall, the boy revealed a rotten front tooth when he smiled. "Five dollars . . . seven with feed."

Glancing at the door, Jack patted the horse's chest. "Somebody here at all times?"

"Yessir."

Jack looked over the space. "Who's here while you're out rustlin' business?"

"That was Uncle Zeke sittin' near the door when we came inside." The boy flashed that rotten tooth again. "Me and my cousin, Ora, take turns keepin' watch overnight."

"The price seems a little—"

"Our prices ensure the best care," the boy said, trying to stand taller. "Come over here and let me show you something."

Jack tied the reins to a rail and followed the boy through the stables.

"We just got this one a few days ago." The boy stopped at a particular stall where a beautiful black horse stood. "What do you think?"

Jack moved his gaze back to the boy. "About what?"

"This horse. What do you think?"

"Look, I ain't got no use for another critter." Jack jutted a thumb toward the door. "Got my hands full with the one I got."

"Oh no." The boy's face soured immediately. "This horse ain't for sale. This here horse belongs to Wild Bill Hickok."

"No kiddin'. So this is the horse that climbed up on the billiard table in Missouri, is it?"

"No sir, Black Nell died a few years back. This one goes by the name Buckshot."

"Wild Bill Hickok . . . here in Deadwood. What do you reckon he's doing here?"

"I ain't got no idea. But it just goes to show how our livery is the most trusted in town."

"Well, if it's good enough for Bill Hickok, then it's good enough for me."

"I'll go fetch my uncle." He started toward the door but turned back. "Oh, what'd you say your name was?"

Jack held his gaze to the horse. "Bill Sutherland."

THE DEADWOOD DEAL

Jack studied his cards as well as the faces of the other players. Perspiration heavied his limbs, causing his shirt to cling to his back and chest. "I'm out," he said, tossing the cards to the table.

The town's streets bustled just outside with a culmination of wagons and horses and what must have been the indistinct murmurings of men, women, and children.

"I heard Bill Hickok is in town." Charles Rich flipped his cards to the table as well. "Reckon he's aiming to get into the gold business?"

"From what I understand, he's here to do some gambling," said a man with a name that escaped Jack. "Heard he has a real knack for poker."

Jack knocked back what whiskey was left in his glass. "I laid eyes on his horse at the livery when I first came into town."

"I wouldn't mind playing a few hands with the man." Charles offered a sneaky smile. "I'd love to someday be able to tell my grandchildren I beat Duck Bill Hickok."

Laughter filled the room.

"I'd be a little more cautious about saying things like that too loudly if I were you." The man Jack couldn't remember a name for shook his head. "It's been said he's got a cantankerous disposition."

Jack rubbed his temples, hoping to quell the burgeoning pressure. "Whereabouts is he set up?"

"From what I was told, he's taken to Nuttall and Mann's Saloon." Charles released his smile. "Heard they're giving him a cut in hopes his fame will draw more lappers."

"You gonna deal, or are we just gonna yammer on about some dime-novel hustler?" The player to Jack's right scrunched up his sweaty face.

"There's no reason to get all worked up, Albert." Charles slid the cards in front of the man. "Here, cut the deck before you keel over with a coronary."

"I just don't understand why we're wasting so much—"

"Then stop wasting time, Albert." Charles gestured toward the cards. "Christ almighty, we're sitting here waiting on *you*!"

After making the cut, the man slid the deck in front of the dealer. "You're makin' me ill as a hornet, Charlie. If you ever get the chance to gamble with Hickok, you should do yourself a favor and keep your dad-blasted mouth shut."

Laughter erupted again.

"Point taken, Albert. Point taken."

The dealer made quick work of distributing the cards.

"Hold on a second." Jack filled his glass again before placing the contents from his pockets onto the table. "It appears I'm running low."

"You talking about your whiskey bottle or money?" Charles squinted toward the pile of items in front of Jack. "How in the world did you get your hands on ghost beads?"

Jack raked them into a closed fist. "Some old woman gave 'em to me while I was ridin' out this way."

"Navajo?"

"She didn't look it to me. But if there was such a thing as a *Loco* tribe, she sure as hell woulda been the queen chief."

Charles held out a hand. "Mind if I take a look?"

"We're wasting time with all the—"

"Good lord, Albert!" Charles turned on his stool. "Does your wife have you on a curfew or something?"

The man's face reddened. "Of course not!"

"Then what in God's name has put you in such a rushed tizzy?"

Albert briefly set his tongue to the corner of his mouth. "Don't mind me. I was just under the impression we were playing poker here."

Charles rolled one of the beads between a forefinger and thumb. "My wife's been searching for a strand of these for well over a year now, but none of the Indians will sell them to us for some reason."

"You should tell her the beads are meant to protect from ghosts and evil," Albert said with a grin. "Not ugly husbands."

Laughter erupted again.

"You willing to part with these?" Charles lifted an eyebrow. "I'll give you five dollars for them right here, right now."

"Five dollars? Are you serious? I had no idea they were worth anything."

"Do we have a deal?"

Jack nodded. "I reckon we do."

"Well I'm sure relieved we got that settled." Albert held up is arms. "Hopefully we can get on with the game now."

THE DEADWOOD DEAL

The young man who first led Jack to the livery sat at the establishment's front doors with a lantern that held back the darkness.

The night air seemed to cut into the soul's quick in spite of an absence of breeze or storm.

Jack finished what was left of his whiskey and tossed the bottle to the side of the walkway.

"You're out and about mighty late, Mister Sutherland." The boy climbed to his feet. "If you're worried about your horse, I can assure you I fed all the animals a few hours ago."

"Just out for a walk and thought I'd stop by and check on things. Gotta make sure the old gal knows I haven't abandoned her or anything."

"Ain't nothin' wrong with that, but . . . " The young man lit another lantern and held it out. "Trust me, you're gonna need this when you go in yonder."

Leather and hay and manure stirred the air, along with shuffling hoof movement and neighs.

The mare stuck her head over the gate and nickered.

"There you are," Jack said. "I wanted to be sure they were carin' for you properly."

The beast nudged into him as he patted its broad neck.

"Sure is a different place 'round these parts, ain't it?" Jack retrieved a carrot from his pocket. "Especially when you ain't got no law houndin' over you."

The horse snorted, stretching toward Jack's hand.

"Oh, you see what I brought you, don't you?" He snapped the carrot into several pieces and held them out in a cold palm. "I know how you love these."

Nibbling gently, the horse inched closer.

"I'm sorry for pushing you all this way." He held his other palm to his forehead, hoping the coolness would ease the ache. "But it looks to me like you're getting rested good and fed well."

Once the carrot was gone, Jack rubbed the sides of the horse's face. "You're all I've got now. From here on out it's just me and you."

A light emerged at the front doorway, bobbing and swaying with each footstep.

"You've done a mighty fine job takin' care of my critter," Jack said, turning toward the approaching figure. "Much obliged."

"I'd love to say it was all my doing," a deep voice said as the man drew closer. "But I'm only here checking on mine as well."

Jack was surprised the rafters didn't graze the man's hat as he walked.

"My apologies. I thought you was the stable boy comin' in."

"Ain't hardly nothing."

Jack immediately recognized the man's features from the drawings of Wild Bill Hickok he'd seen over the last few years. "I'd better let you be about your business."

Nodding, Hickok edged past Jack, moving toward the stall where Buckshot was stabled.

Ain't hardly nothing. The words seemingly implied he didn't take Jack's comments as an insult . . . *or was he really sayin' I wasn't much?*

Just outside the door, the boy peered past Jack, eyes wide. "Did you see him? That was *him*! That was *Bill Hickok* in the flesh."

Handing the lantern to the boy, Jack started back toward the saloon. "Ain't hardly nothin'."

Pushing his hands deep into his pockets, Jack staggered through town kicking dried mud clots as he went along. It was a queer experience as to how quickly the sweltering days could turn so frigid at night.

But it barely fazed the townspeople as the streets bustled with as much activity in the evenings as they did during the heat of the day.

"Could I interest you in some of the finest mining implements available?" John Varnes held out a long-handled shovel while standing next to a tent with items stacked around it. "Why the gold wouldn't stand a chance with you being so well equipped."

"You nearly got me killed with that chair-throwin' stunt you pulled a few days back."

"You sure have a thick skull, don't you?" Varnes set the shovel against the tent wall. "What is it going to take to get you to finally understand you're bulletproof?"

"I'm just lucky that man missed his shot."

Brushing dust from his lapels, Varnes rolled his eyes. "Give me your pistol."

Instinctively putting a hand to his piece, Jack drew his lower lip between his teeth. "Why?"

Varnes held out a hand. "I'd like to settle this once and for all. Now hand it over."

"You plannin' to shoot me?"

"You leave me no choice." He lifted his chin while keeping his gaze fixed. "I want you to know, beyond a shadow of a doubt, that you have nothing to fear."

Jack stepped to the side. "That's all right. I'll take your word for it."

Keeping his hand outstretched, Varnes smirked. "Just give me the Colt and let's get this over with. The sooner it's done, the sooner we can move on without worries."

The searing pangs in Jack's forehead and face dug into his ears. "I ain't giving you my piece. You can forget about that."

"I am sorry, Jack, but I simply cannot allow you to relent to fears of the flesh."

Coldness washed over Jack at the sight of his very own Colt now in Varnes'shand and no longer tucked in his belt. "How'd you—"

"I can ill afford you reneging on our agreement."

Jack held up his hands. "I believe you. I believe."

"If that was the absolute truth, Jack McCall, you would not have a problem with this at all, now would you?"

"Like hell! I don't reckon I'd be comfortable with someone holdin' a pistol on me even if my skin was made of locomotive steel."

Varnes lifted his aim to Jack's head. "Keep your eyes open and on me. I want you to see the whole thing."

The pressure in Jack's bladder was like a knife twisting inside him. "Jesus Christ. Just give me the Colt back."

Varnes smiled. "You'll get it back."

Darkness came almost as quickly as the gun's report.

CHAPTER 9

"**W**AKE UP!"

Jack's head burned like a festering boil.

"Don't act like you can't hear me, boy." Someone was kicking at Jack's foot. "I said get up!"

Sunlight only intensified the pain as Jack tried to open his eyes. "All right. All right."

Searching for the lingering sourness, Jack reached for his side where the shirt clung to his skin with wetness.

"Go on! Get to moving." The man's face was beet red and twisted with rage. "I can't sell a tarnal thing with a vomit-covered drunk passed out in the middle of my goods!"

Climbing to his feet, Jack steadied himself with the shovel handle leaning against the tent. "Sorry." He searched the immediate area. "Let me find my pistol and I'll be on my way."

"Are you still drunk, boy?" The man pointed at Jack's waistline. "It's right there in your belt."

Jack's stomach raged as he put his hand on the revolver's butt and started off down the street. "Sorry for the trouble."

He brought back a dry hand every time he inspected his head and face, which worked miracles in settling his stomach and nerves. The only wetness he could find was the disgorge on his shirt.

Am I losing my wits?

Pulling the Colt from his belt, Jack took a seat at the back of an empty walkway. He opened the revolver's loading gate and turned the cylinder.

Sure enough, one of the cartridges was spent.

I'll be jiggered.

His stomach roiled again as he went back to probing for wounds.

The pain seemed a little worse than usual, but that was more than likely due to the added pressures of an obvious hangover.

"You're looking mighty rough." Charles Rich reached out a hand to help him to his feet. "Are you okay?"

"I'm fine." Jack returned the Colt to his belt and took the outstretched hand. "Just feelin' the effects of last night's bender."

"You certainly appear as though you accomplished quite a bit of bending." Charles gestured toward Jack's shirt. "As well as airin' the paunch."

Pinching at the wet spot, Jack lifted the cold material from his flesh. "I reckon it's been one of them nights."

"I reckon so," Charles said with a laugh. "I wanted to let you know I'm going to Nuttall and Mann's Saloon later to try to get on the same table as Hickok."

"Is that right? I may join you after I get cleaned up."

"Just don't bring Albert." His smile spread into a chuckle. "God knows he'd have Hickok shootin' up the place within a few minutes."

"How'd your wife like the beads?"

Charles pulled the strand from a pocket. "She's helping her sister with a newborn and won't be home for a few more days."

"You really think you can get on a table with Hickok?"

Charles shrugged. "I'm sure gonna give it a shot."

Nuttall and Mann's Saloon was far too quiet despite the multitude of people drinking and milling about. Most patrons were no doubt there just to catch a glimpse of Deadwood's most famous visitor, but at least they were doing so with a drink in hand.

And Wild Bill Hickok certainly did not disappoint—his demeanor was nearly as stoic and intimidating as his immense stature.

Brownish blonde locks hung to his shoulders in twists and waves—a defiant provocation for bloodthirsty savages wanting to carve them from his scalp.

Sitting with his back to the furthest wall, Hickok volleyed his gaze between his cards and movement throughout the saloon.

Jack nestled up close to the bartender and waited for him to finish with another customer.

"What'll it be?" the man finally said, moving some peanuts in front of Jack.

"Give me a bottle of the cheapest whiskey you got."

The bartender smiled. "That bad of a day, huh?"

"You could say that."

The man placed a bottle in front of Jack before wiping out a glass and setting it closer to Jack's hand. "Two bits."

Sliding the coins across the bar top, Jack nodded. "Much obliged."

"I'm pretty good with accents, let me guess . . . " The bartender cocked his head. "You're from . . . Tennessee?"

Jack filled his glass. "Kentucky."

"Ah, I always get the two mixed up." He held out a hand. "Harry Young."

Jack downed his glass before shaking the man's hand. "Good to meet you, Harry. I'm Bill Sutherland." He filled his glass again. "You from these parts?"

"Truth be told, nobody is *from* Deadwood." He wiped the bar top and leaned against it. "I ran away from my home in New York when I was fourteen so I could see the West for myself."

"I reckon that's been a while back." Jack took a drink. "Or so it would seem."

"Eleven years now."

"I bet this place is a whole lot different than New York." Jack chuckled. "I bet you carry a whole lot bigger pistol now than you did back then."

"I don't even own a piece." He shrugged. "Never had a need for one while working here."

"I see." Jack downed what remained in his glass. "They keep one under the bar top so you don't have to buy one for yourself."

"No, that's not the case at all. But I've thought about buying one from time to time. Never know when one could come in handy out here."

Jack filled his glass again. "Probably a good idea."

"Sutherland!" A voice came over the roar of the crowd. "Bill Sutherland!"

Jack couldn't believe he'd overlooked Charles Rich sitting at Hickok's table.

"That's Bill Sutherland," Charles said to the other players. "He could take Morgan's place."

Tobacco smoke settled throughout the room—a tapestry of stagnant gray haze.

"Come join us, Bill!" Charles was grinning like a possum eating sand briars. "Morgan here is leaving the game."

Jack collected the bottle and glass. "Mighty good meetin' you, Harry."

"Same."

At the table, Hickok shuffled the deck while boring his gaze into Jack. "We've met."

Jack glimpsed at Charles before turning back to Hickok. "That's right. At the livery."

"Have a seat." Hickok nodded toward the empty stool. "Anybody that will go the extra mile for their horse is always welcome at my table."

"I ain't too fond of sittin' away from the door," Jack said, easing into the seat. "But I reckon havin' a man of your reputation watchin' my back is good enough."

Sliding the cards to the dealer, Hickok fixed his attention on Jack. "What unit did you serve with?"

"I ain't been in no uniform."

"He looks a bit young to have served." Charles's salesman smile stretched across his face.

"I ain't never served."

"Then where'd you acquire that Army-issued Colt you got in your belt?" Hickok asked.

A bead of sweat trickled Jack's spine. "Friend of my old man gave it to me back in Wyoming."

"Where'd *he* get it?"

Jack cleared his throat and leaned forward. "He told me it was rude to kiss and tell when I asked him that very question."

Laughter erupted with Hickok offering a crooked grin. "Let's get back to the game."

Always welcome at my table. The words kept sloshing through Jack's brain, competing with the abundance of alcohol. *He acts like he owns this table or something.*

The first hour came and went as fast as the whiskey, but Jack's pressured bladder made the second hour seem like it drug on forever.

The dealer's eyebrows lifted with a persistent stare. "Bill?"

An elbow from Charles jolted Jack back to the game.

"What is it?"

The dealer shook his head. "Are you in?"

Downing what was left of his glass, Jack fidgeted with his pouch while still clinging to the empty bottle. "Anyone care to spot me on this hand? I'll repay double tomorrow."

"It *is* tomorrow," Charles said, sparking laughter. "It's pert near two in the morning."

"All right then, I'll repay double later *today*."

Laughter again.

"Here," Hickok said, holding out a small stack of change.

Jack stared at the coinage, warmth filling his cheeks and ears. "Thank you."

"This ain't a loan," Hickok said, pulling back his hand when Jack reached for it. "*This* is for you to get yourself something to eat." He dipped his head slightly. "I'm advising you not to play again until you can cover your losses."

The warmth returned, spread.

Hickok's expression did not falter. "Do you find this agreeable?"

Jack unclenched his teeth. *Thinks he can get rid of me as easy as that.* His stomach grumbled again.

"Well?"

The bottle slipped from Jack's hand and rolled across the tabletop where Charles barely saved it from crashing to the floor.

"All right." Jack jarred the table as he clamored to stand. "I'll get something to eat."

The pancakes were not as thick as the ones Jack's mamma made when he was growing up in Kentucky, but they were nearly twice as big in diameter.

A cast-iron smokiness filled the room from the abundance of frying bacon—along with a sweetness from maple syrup and sorghum.

Low down bottom-feeder.

Taking another bite, Jack gripped the fork so tightly his palm ached.

THE DEADWOOD DEAL

Thinks he can just brush me off that easily—goin' out of his way to humiliate me in front of all them people.

Sunlight spilled across the table, adding warmth where shadows stretched toward every nook and cranny.

"I hope you are finding everything to your satisfaction, sir."

Jack recognized the voice before John Varnes stepped into view. The curious man wore an apron over his gaudy suit while brandishing a dish towel draped over his forearm.

"Why can't you just leave me alone?"

Varnes allowed his smile to soften. "Why, Mr. McCall, are you dissatisfied with our agreement?"

"Keep your voice down," Jack said, scanning the room. "You know I'm going by Bill Sutherland."

Varnes pulled a chair from the table and shrugged. "Please, pardon my error, *Mr. Sutherland.*" He lowered himself into the seat. "But it's time for you to live up to your end of the bargain."

"About that—"

"I think you should be aware of the fact that should you renege on our agreement, the bullets you defied while under the contract will instantly succeed as they would have, had you not been bulletproof."

"What the hell does that even mean?"

With eyebrows lifting, Varnes raised his chin. "It means you will meet your demise the moment you break our compact."

The headache was now in Jack's teeth. "Well I guess I have no choice in the matter, now do I?"

"On the contrary, you made your choice when you signed your mark on the contract."

Jack pushed the remaining portions of pancake around his plate. "Well I still don't know who I'm supposed to be—"

"Shouldn't you follow your own counsel and keep your voice down?"

Jack glared at a few patrons staring from a table on the other side of the room. "I'm tired of you stringin' me along," he continued in a hushed tone. "I just want to be done with it all."

"That's certainly understandable." Varnes pulled the apron over his head. "But you already know the person in question."

"See? That's just the problem. I really *don't* know who the person is."

"I'm not saying you know the person's identity, I'm merely stating that you've met the individual here in Deadwood."

Jack dropped his fork into his plate. "That don't tell me anything, I've met quite a few people while here."

"That's right." Varnes nodded. "But you and this man have even shared a gambling table."

"Well that still doesn't narrow things down for me. I've played poker with a dozen or so folks since coming here."

"That is true." Varnes leaned forward. "But only one of those individuals insulted you in front of the whole saloon. Only *one* of those men treated you like a Judas—offering thirty pieces of silver and advising you to stay away from the table until you can cover your bets."

Jack wanted to stand but remained where he was, his legs now sluggish, heavy. "Hickok."

"That is correct."

"Jesus, Mary, and Joseph." Jack's stomach churned. "You can't be serious."

"Oh I am quite serious."

Jack cleared his throat. "Why are you so hellbent on Hickok?"

"Let's just say there was an incident in Denver." His face twisted with what must have been resentment. "The fool ended up breaking a deal we had agreed upon."

"Hold on a second. Are you telling me Hickok is bulletproof as well?"

"I can assure you of this one thing." His widening smile seemed intended more for himself than for Jack's benefit. "James Butler Hickok is far from bulletproof."

"So what did his contract—"

"I suggest you focus on your own agreement." He sat back, lifted his eyebrows. "But after what Hickok has stolen from you and your family, I'm surprised you're not more eager to see the job through."

"What are you talking about? Are you sayin' Wild Bill killed my father?"

"Your father and Hickok have never been in the same territory at the same time." He moved to his feet, leaving the apron on the table. "On the other hand, it was Hickok who, in cold blood, gunned down your brother in Abilene."

Jack shook his head. "I ain't got no brother."

"Your father never told you about him, but you had a brother."

A queasiness tickled Jack's throat. "That ain't so. I had three sisters when I was growin' up, and that's it. Besides, the old man would have told me otherwise."

"He didn't tell you because he didn't want your mother to find out about your illegitimate sibling."

Jack laughed. "That's crazy. He would have told me about him no matter what."

The smirk on Varnes's face turned into a crooked grin. "You mean like how he told you everything about the men from the gang and what they did together? Or how he confided in you about the dozens of people he'd killed?"

"Dozens?"

Varnes retrieved a cigar from his inside coat pocket. "It's just a shame that Hickok robbed you of any hope you may have ever had in meeting your only brother."

"That doesn't sound right to me." Jack quickly got to his feet. "But what about my old man, do you know who killed my father?"

Lighting the cigar, Varnes eased back into his chair. "I tell you what, *Mister Sutherland*, let's get this ordeal behind us and I promise to tell you everything you want to know as to the death of your father. Is this agreeable?"

CHAPTER 10

THE LIVERY WAS a different place during the day. Sunlight stretched through the gaps of the walls, bringing heat and a heightened sense of barnyard odors.

Jack rubbed his horse's nose while the mare craned her neck toward his hand.

"I ain't got nothin' for you to nibble on this time."

The horse shook its head.

"I know. I know. I'm real sorry. I shoulda brought you an apple or something."

He couldn't get the image of Hickok's smug face out of his head. There was something about the stoic blankness he'd held while he was offering the money.

"We ain't gonna stay here much longer," Jack said, grooming the critter's neck with a brush he'd found nearby. "I promise. But I've got something really important I need to do before we can move on."

The livery boy walked by carrying a flake of hay before entering another stall several feet past, and then, almost immediately, came back out empty handed. The young man didn't so much as look in Jack's direction as he headed toward the front door.

"Get yourself rested up, girl. We're gonna have some miles ahead of us real soon." He rubbed the horse's nose again. "And then things are gonna be different. You'll see."

Was Varnes really telling the truth about a brother Jack had never heard of before? And that Hickok killed him in cold blood?

Should've asked what the brother's name was.

A small breeze whistled through the cracks in the planked walls, carrying grit and grime, as well as stirring hay and odors.

"She's well mannered," the boy said, pushing past Jack with a couple more hay flakes. "Most of the time the horses are ornery or demanding."

Jack stepped aside from being startled. "I'd like to take credit for that, but to be right honest about it, she's never been a lick of trouble."

The boy scattered the hay on the dirt floor and checked the water. "Uncle Zeke says feeding from the floor makes 'em healthier. Says it helps drain their noses so they can breathe better."

"Is that right?"

"Yessir. I reckon he knows just about everything there is to know about horses and mules and such." A prideful smile stretched across his face. "Why I bet Uncle Zeke knows more about 'em than anybody."

The horse munched on the hay without movement or noise.

"Sounds like your uncle has taught you quite a bit." Jack placed the brush back on the ledge. "Has he taught you any shoein' skills?"

"Not yet, but he says we'll get around to it someday. I've watched him so many times I could probably do it with my eyes closed, though."

Jack cut off a piece of plug tobacco and crammed it into his mouth. "My grandfather tried to teach me how to shoe when I was a boy back on the farm in Kentucky."

"What do you mean he *tried* to teach you?"

Jack worked the tobacco a bit before situating it into his cheek. "Well I reckon he stopped tryin' because it didn't take."

"What happened?"

"Apparently I wasn't too good at it and the old man feared I would end up injuring one of the poor critters and he'd have to put it down."

"Makes sense."

"He did teach me something I was good at, though." Jack moved the tobacco to his other cheek. "I was real good at killing the hogs for slaughter."

"Yeah?"

"I remember grandpa bragging to anybody who'd listen about how there wasn't a soul alive who could put one down any better than me."

"Saw my daddy kill one before. That thing screamed and squealed like nothing I've ever seen or heard."

Jack nodded. "You gotta know where and how to shoot it. This ain't like waitin' out buffalo, you see. Pigs only sit still without movin' when they're either sleepin' or eatin' or drinkin'. So I always started preparing for the kill the day before."

The boy perched himself on a nearby railing. "What do you mean?"

"You don't want to give 'em any water the day before. That's the key, you get 'em good and parched. Then the next day, while they're drinkin' their fill, you walk right up on 'em and lay a bead an inch or so up from between their eyes." Jack shook his head. "Nary a squeal or a scream—they never know what hit 'em."

"So while they're focused on quenching their thirst, you shoot 'em when they're not paying attention to anything else."

Jack spit. "You could even put the rifle's muzzle right against the poor thing's thick skull if you wanted and it wouldn't pay you no more mind than a worn-out fence post."

"That's pretty smart."

"It ain't shoein', but it's somethin', that's for sure." Jack rubbed the mare's neck. "I reckon I better let you get back to work 'fore your uncle catches you sittin' around in here and gives you what for."

It seemed to be a bustling late afternoon at Nuttall and Mann's Number Ten Saloon, where the rumbling of many voices spilled out onto the street where Jack paced.

The front window revealed that although a number of the usuals were already set up at the back table, Hickok was nowhere to be found.

Of all times for him not to show up.

Wiping sweat from his forehead, Jack moved across the street to keep out of sight while taking note of who went in or came out.

It was funny how a place named Deadwood was actually the liveliest place in the territories, with dozens of miners and fortune seekers arriving in town every day.

It didn't take long before Hickok came down the planked walkway, weaving through the populace, heading for Nuttall and Mann's. He paused a second or two at the door and adjusted his hat before entering.

Jack scrambled across the street to peek through the window. Inside, Hickok had a short conversation with someone at the bar before heading to the back table where a game was already in progress.

THE DEADWOOD DEAL

As the legendary gunman approached the game, the player sitting with his back to the door rose and gestured that Hickok could take his place as he was leaving.

Hickok then appealed to Charles Rich to trade seats so he could sit facing the door, but Charlie refused. He apparently asked again—and again, Charlie refused. Jack couldn't hear the conversation from the window, but it was obvious that's what was being discussed.

Removing his jacket, Hickok finally pulled the stool out from the table with his foot and sat as the game seemingly picked up right where it left off.

This is as good as it's going to get.

Scanning the patrons and activity of the entire saloon, Jack focused on the hands dealt at the table, and waited for Hickok's shoulders to slouch with complacency.

Someone brushed against Jack's arm while opening the door to go inside. Jack quickly followed, slowly making his way toward the bar.

The rambunctious crowd noise did little in the way of drowning out the pulsing heart in his nose and face, or quelling the misery that accompanied it.

Nodding to Harry Young as he approached the bar, Jack couldn't figure out what to do with his hands. The very thought of acting normal only made things worse.

Just get on with it.

Averting his gaze, Jack slowly moved down the length of the bar and paused where the gold-weighing scales rested at the end.

Coldness expanded in Jack's chest when Hickok turned toward the bar and said, "Bring me fifty dollars worth of checks, Harry."

Jack didn't move, the coldness quickly spreading to his legs and feet.

Harry placed the stack on the table in front of Hickok and waited just off to his side.

Hickok gazed up at him, gesturing toward a player Jack didn't recognize. "The old duffer broke me on that hand."

Jack's first step was wobbly as he made a beeline for the table. Each succeeding footstep felt like the quick, jarring paces made when drunk.

The coldness turned to fire as perspiration beaded his forehead, threatening to move into his eyes.

Stepping just behind Hickok, Jack brought the piece from his belt and aimed it mere inches from Wild Bill's head.

The recoil and report startled Jack as much as it apparently did everyone else.

"Damn you, take that!"

Gasps and grumbles erupted, along with a piercing ring, as Jack stepped back and surveyed the room.

The crowd went silent at the sight of Hickok's slumping body, as well as Jack's smoking pistol. They were all on their feet now, focusing solely on Jack, faces rife with confusion and fear and anger.

Waving his Colt around as a warning, Jack eased his way to the back door before taking off down the alley where he found, to his surprise, a tethered horse a few feet away.

He released the reins, put a foot in the stirrup, and tried pulling himself up by the saddle horn, but the whole rig slid from the horse as he fell to the ground.

Clambering to get back to his feet, Jack recovered his Colt and scrambled down the alley away from all the shouting and commotion.

In addition to his ringing ears, aching face, and the unbearable heat, Jack's gut churned and rumbled with threats of regurgitation.

The clamoring and shouting drew closer, louder. It was evident that many of those from the saloon were following in an attempt to apprehend Wild Bill Hickok's killer.

Slipping through an open back door, Jack found himself in the darkened storage area of a butcher's shop, and locked the door behind him. The coppery scent reminded him of his early years helping his grandfather butcher the hogs he'd killed.

"You always want to take your time when stickin' and guttin'," his grandfather would say while working on the carcass. "One poor move of the blade and you can ruin the meat."

There must have been a search party just outside with yelling and running and shuffling about.

"You clearly have not lost your touch," John Varnes said, stepping out from the shadows wearing a bloodstained butcher's apron. "Congratulations on fulfilling the deal."

Jack moved closer. "Our business is all done with and I'm gettin' the hell outta here."

"And you certainly deserve it." Varnes wiped his blood-mucked hands on the apron. "How does it feel to have finally avenged your brother's death?"

"I told you, I ain't got no brother!"

"My boy, if you know what's good for you, you'll embrace the loss of your brother."

"I've had enough of this." Jack pointed a finger at Varnes. "I did exactly what you asked, now get me outta here."

"Excuse me?"

"Get me outta here!"

Shaking his head, Varnes offered a weird smile. "You know quite well that that is not part of the contract."

The growing chaos outside seemed to close in on Jack as coldness returned to his chest and stomach. "No," he said, raising the Colt to Varnes's head. "I don't care what it takes, just get me the hell outta here!"

"I honestly do not understand why someone who is bulletproof can be so concerned about a horde of men chasing with bullets and anger."

Jack cocked the hammer. "I ain't gonna tell you again."

"Pull the trigger." Varnes's face was icy. "Or better yet, since you don't think you're going to get out of here alive, why don't you put the muzzle to your own head and end it now."

"Listen—"

"Why give those bloody mongrels the satisfaction? If you *truly* do not believe to be bulletproof, or that you will not make it out of this building alive, then do the deed yourself and be done with it."

The crowd noise was growing outside.

"But if you turn that revolver on yourself and you come out unscathed, well then what do you have to worry about?"

Jack lowered his piece. "I'm not afraid to die."

Someone attempted to open the door from outside. "This one's locked as well!"

Gesturing toward Jack's Colt, Varnes nodded. "Prove to yourself once and for all. Or take from them the very thing they seek."

A commotion came from the front side of the butcher's shop this time.

Jack lifted the muzzle to his temple and cocked the hammer. "I'm not afraid to die."

"Then stop being afraid to live!"

Jack closed his eyes and pulled the trigger to an empty click. He peeked a bit while thumbing back the hammer and pulling the trigger again . . . to yet another empty click. He began laughing as he went through the motions three more times . . . all to empty clicks. "I really *am* bulletproof," he said. But Varnes was no longer with him.

Another ruckus came from the front again as several men burst into the storage area. "There he is!"

Jack was still laughing when the men wrestled him to the ground.

"I said to wake up!" Someone jostled Jack's shoulder. "We ain't got all day, now move it."

Trying to sit upright from his side, Jack struggled with getting his arms to cooperate. "What's goin' on?"

"Here." A hand pulled Jack's arm to move him into a sitting position. "We've gotta get you to your trial."

The binding on Jack's wrists left reddened skin and an irritating fire. "Trial?"

"That's right. You killed Wild Bill Hickok yesterday, remember?" The man's face was red and sweaty. "Or were you too drunk to even remember?"

"Who are you?"

"Joseph Brown." The man used both hands under Jack's arm to pull him to his feet. "I'm the new sheriff."

"What town are you taking me to?"

Brown turned Jack toward the door. "Your trial is going to take place at the theater."

"Now hold on a second, I thought there weren't no law in Deadwood."

Brown shook his head. "There wasn't any until you done what you did. A bunch of us got pulled into duties we never asked for. I was appointed sheriff for this ordeal, thank you very much."

There were a few armed men waiting outside who took up walking with the sheriff and Jack. "Just so you know, this here trial and everything was thrown together so the townspeople wouldn't string you up on the spot."

Men and women watched as Jack and the new lawmen made their way through the middle of the street.

"Just keep your head down so we can get you there with no bullet holes or neck burns."

Jack laughed.

"I'm glad *you* think it's funny." He squeezed Jack's bicep while continuing to pull him ahead. "Because me and these men are risking our necks to ensure you make it safely to trial, you jackass!"

The faces of the gawking people gave the impression they were saddened or tired. Not one of them tried to intervene or intercept, but just in front of the theater, a smile stood out like a fiddle in a box of mouth harps.

"There's Varnes," Jack said, stretching his neck to get a better view.

"Shut up." Brown jerked Jack's arm forward. "We're almost there."

Varnes offered an open-palm wave before disappearing into the crowd.

Jack couldn't get over how quiet the crowd was—no screaming or yelling or throwing things like he'd seen with captured fellas in the past.

"When we get inside, I want you to keep your mouth shut until it's your turn to speak." Brown kept his gaze in front of him. "Understood?"

"Who's the judge?"

"I just told you to keep your mouth shut until it's your turn to speak!"

Jack tried to stop walking but found himself pulled forward again. "You said *when we get in there*! If my eyes aren't deceiving me, we ain't in there yet!"

"The judge's name is William Kuykendall."

"Well with a name like that, I can sure understand why you was avoiding the question."

"And does the defense have any other witnesses to call?"

The lawyer next to Jack rose. "Yes, Your Honor. If it pleases the court, we would like to call the defendant to the stand."

The spectators broke into excessive murmuring and chattering.

Taking the chair just to the right of the judge, Jack crossed his arms and squinted past the numerous stage lamps reflected on him. It was as though he was standing in mid-July heat right next to a brush fire.

"It's been pointed out by the prosecution that your name really isn't Bill Sutherland." The lawyer meandered about with as much showmanship as any actor the very stage had previously graced. "But that your given name is John McCall."

"Jack."

"That's right, your preference is *Jack* McCall." The lawyer pulled back the side-front of his jacket to place a dramatic hand on his hip. "And there's a very good reason you went by an alias, correct?"

"That's right."

"Would you kindly explain as to why you took use of this other name?"

"Survival."

"Please explain to the court what you mean by that, and testify as to what happened."

Uncrossing his arms, Jack leaned forward. "Well, men, I have but few words to say. Wild Bill killed my brother, and I killed him." He straightened a bit. "Wild Bill threatened to kill me if I crossed his path, and I'm not sorry for what I did. As a matter of fact, I'd do the same thing over again!"

The murmuring and chattering swelled again, this time louder than before.

"All right, that's enough," the judge called out as he rose from his seat. "Keep it down! We're still in session."

A quietness came over the auditorium with the exception of faint shuffling in the crowd.

Turning to the lawyer on the other side of the stage, the judge lifted his hands. "The witness is yours."

The man rose just briefly enough to state, "The prosecution rests, your honor."

"How long has it been?" Jack shifted his rear on the floor.

"Hard to tell." Sheriff Brown stared back from a chair next to the door. "Been hours, I'm sure of that much."

"What do you reckon they're gonna do?"

Shrugging, Brown pushed his hat back on his head. "I ain't got no idea. A lot of folk wants you dead for what you did, but I think a bunch of others are a little more understanding after hearing about your brother."

Jack fiddled with the rope around his wrists. "I reckon we'll know one way or another 'fore too long."

"You don't seem too flustered for a man standing trial for murder."

"Ain't much to fret about. Won't do any good anyways."

"That's a bold way of looking at it." He offered a nod. "Especially for someone who could be facing the noose."

"Ain't worried about that at all."

"You don't think they'll hang you if they find you guilty?"

"I ain't worried if they do." He gave a slight grin. "I can't die."

"What in God's name do you mean by that?"

Chuckling, Jack leaned back against the wall. "I reckon you'll see."

"I'm not playing any games with you, McCall. I'm not about to put my neck on the line, or the necks of any of the other men for that matter, to keep you safe just so you can do something stupid and get us all killed."

"You ain't got nothin' to worry about with me, constable. No sir, I ain't about to make trouble for anybody."

"That's what I want to hear." He adjusted his holster and crossed his legs. "Now what are you talking about when you say you can't die?"

"I mean exactly that, I can't die." He took in a deep breath and released it. "It's a long story, and you won't believe it no ways."

"Now you need to—"

The knock at the door caused Brown to wince.

"They're ready," a voice sounded from the other side.

"All right, McCall, let's get moving." He helped pull Jack to his feet. "You better not be scheming up anything. You hear me?"

"You ain't gonna have to worry about me."

"Has the jury reached a verdict?"

A man among the secluded jurors rose to his feet. "We have, Your Honor."

"What say you?"

The man straightened himself. "After nearly twelve hours of—"

"We're not looking for any formalities or lengthy expository, all I want to hear is *guilty* or *not guilty*. You understand?"

Nodding, the man stared forward. "Not guilty."

The crowd erupted with yelling and gasps and grumblings, shifting and moving about as they shoved one another within the confines of the hall.

"Order!" The judge banged a block of wood against the table in front of him. "I will have order in this court!"

As the crowd started settling, the judge turned to the sheriff. "Get him to the back somewhere. Cut him loose, but keep him there until I get a chance to come back and speak with him."

The back stage area was dark and empty and smelled of paint, tobacco smoke, and lamp oil.

"Does that mean I'm free?"

Brown led Jack into a cramped room in the far corner. "That's right, but you heard the judge say he wants to speak to you before we let you go."

"But I'm free?"

Nodding, Brown began cutting the rope from Jack's wrist. "Jury found you not guilty, so yes, you're free."

Jack rubbed the rope burns once the ties were cut away. "Are you stayin' on as sheriff now that this trial is over?"

"Hell no." He peeked out the door for a moment. "Going back to digging gold as soon as I can."

The crowd noise was faint from the distance, but still very much active.

"Well I wish you all the luck in the world. I really do. You've been nothing but fair and decent to me during this whole ordeal."

"Tell me something." Brown scratched at his beard. "What did you mean when you said you couldn't die?"

Jack smiled. "Let's just say I made a deal and now I can't die."

"What exactly do you mean you made a deal?"

"I know it sounds—"

"There you are." The door opened as the judge stepped inside. "I believe we have everyone calmed down and out the door." The man's ruddy face glistened with perspiration. "Thank you for everything, Joseph. You served honorably as sheriff during this fiasco."

"I'd like to say the pleasure was all mine, but I think you know I would not be telling the truth."

"And for you, Mr. McCall." He turned toward Jack with a stern face. "If you know what's best for you, you'd head out of Deadwood as quickly as possible."

"I plan to do just that."

"Good. We'll have your horse saddled and brought over once it gets a little darker." He touched Jack's chest with an index finger. "Once you're on that horse, you're on your own, boy."

After nearly a month on the run, Jack made his way to Wyoming—first to Cheyenne before moving on to Laramie.

The first saloon he came to in town was a bit larger than those in Deadwood, but nowhere near as busy or raucous.

"Give me a whisky," he said, placing a few coins on the bar top.

"You got it." The bartender took down a bottle from the back shelf and poured. "You look familiar."

"Been through here a time or two."

"That seems to be the case with everyone." The man corked the bottle and moved it to the side. "Seems like everybody just stops by Laramie on their way to wherever they are going."

"Oh? And why is that?"

"I reckon the rocky dirt makes it damn near impossible to properly set roots." He smiled. "It's easier to travel across, than to dig into, I suppose."

"So why are you here?"

"I'm saving up enough money to head out to Deadwood and see if I can't find me some of that gold everybody's talking about."

Jack knocked back the whiskey and slid the glass forward. "Give me another."

The bartender refilled. "Where you headed?"

"Anywhere but Deadwood."

"I heard somebody killed Wild Bill Hickok out there."

"You heard correctly." Jack downed the whiskey, jutted a thumb to his chest. "And you're lookin' at the feller who shot him."

The man stared blankly. "No fooling?"

"That's right. Son of a bitch killed my brother and said he'd kill me if he ever got the chance. But I was acquitted of all charges by a court of law."

"I reckon a fella has to be pretty dang quick to kill Wild Bill Hickok."

Nodding toward the empty glass, Jack slid a few more coins across the bar. "You don't have to be quick when you're quiet."

He stopped pouring the whiskey and scrunched up his face. "You mean . . ."

"Keep pourin'." Jack gestured toward the glass. "Listen, when a practiced killer says he's gonna gun you down, you better believe every word he says." He gulped the whiskey and ran a sleeve across his mouth. "And if you wanna live, then you better beat him to the draw . . . no matter how you do it."

"So what'd you and your brother do to put Wild Bill Hickok on your scent?"

Placing the glass on the bar, Jack studied the man's face. "What?"

"Why was Wild Bill after the two of you in the first place?"

"Well . . . " His gaze roamed the saloon. "I reckon he just wanted to kill somebody."

The man placed the bottle back on the shelf. "Uh huh."

"Whereabouts is the nearest livery?"

"If I was you, I'd keep moving. And if not, I wouldn't go around bragging about what you did in Deadwood." He wiped out Jack's glass and placed it under the bar top. "I don't think folks around here will take too kindly to your story."

Taking a step back, Jack lowered his hand near the Colt. "I can take care of myself."

Jack spread his cards on the table and smiled. "I hope you fellers don't mind, but I brought some ladies to the dance." He scooped the money from the center of the table. "Three queens have never looked so lovely."

Groans and grumbles came as cards landed at the table's center.

"Jack McCall?" the voice said from behind him.

As he turned to look up, Jack felt someone jerking the Colt from his waistband. "Hey!"

Two men dragged him from the chair by his arms. "Put the shackles on him."

"What's this all about?" Jack tried pulling away. "I ain't done nothin' but played cards."

"You're under arrest, McCall." A big fella stepped in front of him.

"Arrest? For what?"

"For the murder of James Butler Hickok."

"I was acquitted! Ain't you heard?" He tried pulling away again. "The jury declared I was not guilty."

"Make sure he doesn't have any other guns or anything." The man turned to Jack. "I'm Deputy Marshal Balcomlie. And the jury you mentioned was just as illegal as the court itself."

"What the hell are you talkin' about?"

"There's no law in Deadwood, son. And that's because the town is illegally set up inside Indian territory that was established by the federal government."

"That can't be right. There was a judge and lawyers and—"

"All illegal." The marshal pulled at the shackles on Jack's wrists. "But you're fixin' to stand trial in a real courtroom."

"At least let me take my winnings." Jack nodded toward the table. "I just won a bunch of money. Hell, I'd be willin' to share if you'd let me go."

The marshal pulled him toward the door. "Son, you ain't gonna need any money with where you're going."

"Where are you taking me?"

"We'll be leaving for Yankton as soon as your preliminary hearing is over here in town."

Jack took in the darkness when they finally made it outside. "Wild Bill killed my brother, you know. Said he was gonna kill me too, but I beat him to the punch."

"You know damn well, you don't have a brother, McCall." Balcomlie jerked at the shackles. "You've been too stupid to realize all your bragging about it would catch up with you."

"I'm telling you a man named John Varnes hired me to kill Hickok over some dispute the two of them had in Denver."

The jail cell was small, dark, and carried what must have been the smells of past sins.

"And I told you we sent someone to Deadwood about that." The attorney pushed his shoulders up to his cheeks. "And there's nobody there by that name."

"There's gotta be something we can do."

Placing a hand on Jack's shoulder, the lawyer shook his head. "I'm afraid unless we get some kind of a miracle, or a stay of execution from the governor, the jury has found you guilty and the judge has set your date."

Jack gazed at the ceiling. "Well I sure didn't think about all of this when I agreed to the deal."

"I'm sorry? What deal are you referring to?"

"It don't matter now, I reckon." He gently rubbed his forehead. "Say, how long do they leave a feller hangin' 'fore they cut him down?"

"Your sentence states the guilty party is hanged by the neck until dead. So it depends on how long that takes, I imagine."

Jack sat forward. "What happens if the feller gettin' hanged doesn't die?"

"I'm not sure I understand your question."

"Oh just forget about it. We'll get there when we get there."

The lawyer rose to his feet. "Unfortunately, I have a great deal of paperwork to finish. But if I'm not mistaken, they have a priest who wants to speak with you if you'd like."

"I don't want no damn priest in here."

Shrugging, the lawyer moved toward the hall. "Suit yourself."

The bars clanged shut, leaving a ringing in Jack's ears. Dripping echoed from somewhere without a sign of water or dampness.

He rubbed again at his throbbing forehead, working to ease the pressure. Closing his eyes, Jack found the flashing colors and lights he'd been used to for a while.

"Bless you, my son," John Varnes said, stepping in front of the bars. He was adorned with a priest's robe and a crucifix around his neck. "I have come to hear your confession."

Rising from the threadbare cot, Jack took a step forward. "Damn you, Varnes. Get me outta here!"

"My boy, how many times must I tell you that that was never in our agreement? I've merely stopped by to tell you goodbye."

Jack grasped the bars as he moved his face closer. "Don't you see what they're planning to do?" The heat in his neck spread to his cheeks. "They're gonna hang me!"

"There is no question about that, I'm afraid."

"And you're okay with that? You don't care a bit in the world that they are going to string me up just like that?"

"I have no say in the matter, I'm afraid."

"*You're* the reason I'm in this mess!"

"That's not true." Varnes quietly put his hands behind his back. "You are in this mess because *you* failed to take precautions in not getting caught."

Leaning his aching head against the bars, Jack stared into Varnes. "Don't you see what's going to happen? They are going to string me up and leave me hanging there for . . . who knows how long before they realize I can't die!"

Varnes scrunched his eyebrows together. "What did you say?"

"You heard me!"

"I fear you have misunderstood our agreement. The contract you signed only stated that you would be *bulletproof*." He shook his head. "It most certainly did *not* state that you would be deathless."

ELIJAH'S ELIXIR

KEITH LANSDALE

"COULD YOU LIMP more?"

"I don't got a bum leg, Boss," he said. "I'm doing the vision thing."

I looked him over.

"I just think a limp would be better."

I jumped off the cart and drug one foot behind me.

"I know what a limp looks like," he said. "I just don't think that's what I want to do."

"The way you move looks too . . . " I thought a moment. "Healthy."

Luther was the wrong man to play feeble. He was a giant. His muscles had muscles. And he moved like he could eat a mountain and shit a hill, but he was who I had.

"I just need more people to witness it," I said. "They cannot see your vision improve. But they can see a limp vanish before their very eyes."

"The whole thing just feels dishonest." Luther walked over to the cart and slapped one of the kegs. "Why not just really cure someone?"

"You are aware of how this works," I said. "Sometimes it takes time, and I need them to see immediate results. And it does us both no good if we cannot convince them to try it. You are a fan of getting paid, right?"

Luther nodded.

"And you are proof it works," I said. "Plus, you have seen time and time again what this can do."

"It did make me stronger."

"But it does not happen right away. It needs time."

"I reckon you're right, Boss," he said. He took off his straw hat and rubbed the side of his head where a scar marked him. I had never asked what had been the cause, and he had never offered.

"We just need to put on a little bit of a show to get it in their hands," I said. "It is just a little innocent exaggeration that helps us all."

Luther leaned in silence and let the idea roll around in his head. A low-flying bird caught his eye as it darted across the campsite where we had stopped our wagons. A secluded spot a ways outside the town of Shadybrook. Tall trees cut the area sharply between us and the main road that led into town. Not that we were hiding, mind you. It was just best to be out of reach.

Luther produced the stub of a cigar and stuck it in the corner of his mouth.

"We talked about flames around the elixir," I said.

"I know, Boss," he said. "I know. I'm just chewing on it."

He was still in his thoughts.

"And the elixir helped Rose?"

"It didn't help me do shit," Rose said. Then she reconsidered. "I take that back. It did help me take a shit."

Rose had her talismans and trinkets spread out across a couple wooden planks in front of her for a makeshift table. She did not even look up, her long red hair draped in front of her face as she laid a tarot card in front of her, stared at it, and laid down another.

"She is just mad because it did not make her any more appealing," I said.

Rose looked up from her cards, ready to make a snide retort.

"Someone is approaching," she said.

"Does it say so in the cards?" Luther said.

"As always, I'm the only one who can see," she said. "Maybe your vision really is bad."

She pointed toward a break in the trees where a small, young man pushed his way out and into the clearing. The bushes and trees snapped back in place behind him like swaying green curtains. One caught his boot and sent him into the dirt.

Luther tried to make himself scarce. He pulled his hat down low in front of his face and walked to the other side of the cart, which was about as effective as hiding an elephant in an open field.

The young man realized he had been seen and gave a wave as he rose to his feet.

"What can we do for you, good sir?" I yelled out and juggled between friend or foe. He was empty-handed, which gave some comfort.

"I thought you might be back here," he said.

"We certainly are," I said. "And, again, I ask, what can we do for you?"

He never broke stride and smiled from ear to ear the whole time he approached.

"I've been looking for you," he said. "They call me Little Bill. I've been catching rides with travelers, as no one will sell me a horse, hoping to catch up with you. I heard you had been in One Stone, but by the time I got there, they said you were already headed to Tusom. Got there, you were headed to Bakersville. It seems like no matter how fast I'd be, you'd be gone before I arrived. I feel mighty foolish, as I have been trying to catch up to you since you left Shadybrook in the spring. And here I finally do, and you're about to be back where I . . . "

He trailed off, and the smile went away.

"That is quite the story, Little Bill," I said, and looked to see what had fascinated him so. He and Luther were staring right at each other.

"Last few places described you helping a big man," Bill said. "Someone they had never seen before. Large man, scar near his eye."

Luther ducked away, far too late.

"I can still see you," Bill said.

"No you can't," Luther said.

"Well, we did cure Luther," I said. "And he jumped on the payroll to do some of the heavy lifting."

Bill looked conflicted.

"But last few towns—"

"Want me to read your future," Rose interrupted. This time I was happy she chimed in. "Tell you maybe of riches? Women?"

Little Bill abandoned his turmoil and looked at Rose intrigued.

"You know my future?"

"Little man, I know everything," she said and shuffled her deck, "Future, past, and everything in between."

"What will it cost me?" he said as he took a few steps toward Rose.

I stood nearby, always curious to see her work.

"A half-dollar won't make you taller," Rose said, "but it may save your life."

She produced an empty can from beneath her robes and thrust it toward him. He reached into his pocket.

"That seems a little high," he said. "What about half a half dollar?"

"What about half a half reading?"

"Deal," he said, and dropped the coin in the can.

Rose pulled the can back, and it vanished beneath her robes. She picked up the cards and shuffled them a time or two.

"Does it say I'm going to be rich?" he said. He edged closer as the cards spun and flapped together, like a bird's wings taking flight.

"Spirits don't work like that," she said with another shuffle of the cards. "They tell me what they want to tell me."

"Ask them spirits if I'm going to be rich," he said.

She gave him a look and pulled a card from the deck and slapped it between them.

They looked down to see THE FOOL.

He looked up.

"I'm no fool," he said.

"Cards have meaning," she said. "That can stand for many things. You. Someone you know. Someone you don't know."

"Well, that seems a little convenient," he said.

She turned another card. THE SUN.

I looked at the card hoping to interpret its meaning. Just looked like a child on a horse with a big sun in the background.

"What's that one mean?"

"As I've said, they have meaning," Rose said. "But until they've all been laid out, the spirit's message is not clear."

Another card turned. TEN OF SWORDS.

Rose abruptly looked up at him.

"So, what's that one mean?" he said. "That mean something good?"

"Sure," she staggered and picked up her cards. "Spirits are saying you're going to die a happy man."

"And rich?" He leaned on her makeshift table as he asked.

Rose stood up and gathered the rest of her things.

"Why not?" she said. "A rich, happy man."

Rose put the last of her trinkets away and went up the little steps and into her wagon and pulled them up behind her. Never seen her end a reading like that. It made the hair on my neck stand on end.

"I knew it," he said and turned to me. "I knew I was gonna be rich. God had told me so."

"Wonderful to hear," I said and put my arm around his shoulders. "But you never finished telling me why it was you have been scouring the world for me."

He almost jumped, reminded of his original mission.

"The people in Shadybrook," he said, "they need your help."

It was still early the next morning as our wagons bumped along. Luther was up front with me where he drove the horses, with Little Bill pressed between us. There was usually enough room for three people, but Luther was a man and a half at least, so Bill was getting acquainted.

We were back on the well-traveled road between towns, so it was not a tough ride. The wagon still shook side to side, as if keeping time, and the things inside clanged around making noises like an old clock in need of a tune-up. We could hear the river rush not too far away, a little more than usual, which led me to believe there was a possible storm upstream. There were moments in the trees between us and the river I had seen movement, but every time I tried to discover the source, there was nothing but the green of leaves that swayed in the wind's rhythm.

Our lead wagon was impossible to be mistaken. A picture of my face which donned my large black top hat, and the words, "Elijah's Elixir," in faded paint. It might be time for a change. I had never liked the name Elijah when I picked it, but it sounded right.

Attached to our wagon was the cart filled with the kegs, and behind that was Rose who drove her own wagon. She gripped the reins of her horses and stayed a bit of a distance from us. She had not spoken a word after her reading the day before and had been silent as we packed up this morning, and that did keep me off kilter. She never took her eyes off our new companion.

Little Bill rubbed his hands together.

"You all good there, Bill?" I said.

Bill snapped away from what had his mind occupied and sort of nodded.

"Just not sure what happens now," he said. "It just sat with me that finding you was the easy part, and it wasn't easy."

The wagon continued to knock around, keeping time.

"Little Bill, I am happy you came to find us," I said. "Though I admit I am befuddled by what you explained."

"I'm befuddled, too," Little Bill said. "And I'm the one explaining it."

Bill rubbed his hands together again, back in his thoughts.

"Everything you said about your mama," he said. "It just let me know that someone like that . . . Plus you being so smart . . . "

It seemed Bill could not find the end of his own thoughts.

"Well, I appreciate the kind words," I said. The stories about my mother did help move the elixir, but it hurt to tell them. I was just ready to unload the rest of these kegs and live a quiet life somewhere.

Normally, I would have dropped Luther before town to let him blend into the crowd, but Bill had ruined those plans. But he may have brought us something better. If the people of Shadybrook wanted me here, that meant there was an opportunity to offer my services. Though I had not quite settled on what those services may be, or what they may cost.

The town was never much to talk about. Shops on either side of the main road, a bucket hung over a well not too far off in the distance, and a large bronze statue of a man that stood in the middle holding an object up to the light, like it was being offered to the sun. It was not clear who the statue memorialized, or what it held, but it only had the one arm.

But unlike before, there was no movement. No sounds of talk and laughter. No one stood near the shops. No music came from the saloon. Just a lot of nothing.

A big sign arched over the road that read, "Welcome To Shadybrook." Though the paint used to do so was faded even worse than my wagon's. A round man with bright red cheeks was laying belly up on the side of the road, like a dead deer bloated in the sun. He heard us bump closer and stirred. He started the process of getting to his feet, which was no small task, though a man of his size, nothing was.

Luther slowed the horses just as the large man got his feet under him, and he leaned against the cart for support, and to catch his breath. Standing had knocked the wind out of him.

"Welcome," he wheezed, "to Shadybrook," and wheezed again. "But we ain't allowing strangers into . . . " he stopped. "That you Little Horsefucker?

Bill had almost disappeared into the mountain that was Luther.

"It is," Bill said.

"This them?"

"It is," Bill said.

"Well, hell, I thought so," the fat guy said. "Has that hat just like you said. I'm Tommy Clifton. Sheriff 'round these parts."

"What happened to Sheriff Boyd?" I said.

"That's exactly what we can't figure out," he said. "We ain't exactly missing him or nothing. Boyd was a sour apple for sure. But we can't figure out what happened to him."

"Little Bill—" I started.

"Little Horsefucker," Tommy interjected.

"Yes . . . " I said with hesitation. "He said something about people vanishing. And some livestock."

"We were wondering if maybe it was just—" Luther started, but Tommy did not let him finish.

"I know what you're thinking," Tommy said and pulled a biscuit from his pocket. "C'Yotes or something getting them."

As he bit into the biscuit, crumbs tumbled down onto his ill-fitted shirt where he had pinned the familiar sheriff star.

"Coyotes was among our guesses, yes," I said.

"You got another one of those biscuits?" Luther said.

He chewed and chewed, then audibly swallowed. "I do."

"Can I have one?"

"You may not."

Luther slumped back against the wagon.

"Like I was saying, Jim Brown, guy who had 'bout 50 head of cattle. Told us he'd seen one vanish. Right in front of his eyes. He was keep'n us up on the count dropping. When he got to 'round 32, then, well, no more Jim Brown."

"No more Jim Brown," I repeated. I turned to Bill, then back to Tommy. "But I am still quite muddled why anyone would come in search of myself. I am no lawman. Though I pride myself on the effectiveness of my wares, and it is true I do possess other abilities, though I do not believe that makes me any more qualified than—"

"Tommy!" screamed a woman from down the road. "Another one's gone!"

A woman, wearing an apron with her hair up in a bun, had some hurry in her step, but the limp she walked with added to the movement, and she clocked in at the speed of general concern at best.

She looked over our wagons as she got closer and noticed Bill. "Oh, Bill!" she said. "You're back!"

"Horsefu—," Tommy started, but the woman backhanded him in the chest.

"Don't you use that language around me, Tommy," she said. "I remember when you were knee high to the horse that . . . "

She looked over at Bill.

"I'm just glad you're back," she said. "And this must be the brilliant scientist you were talking about."

"This is him, Miss Cutty," Bill said.

I looked around, and half expected to find someone else.

"Madam, I believe my qualifications might be inflated," I said. "While I am a man of many talents, a scientist, I have never claimed to be."

"Don't be modest," Bill said. "You were telling us all how you found this concoction when you tried to save your mother. And while you might not have fancy degrees, you're certainly a man of great intelligence."

"Ha!" The first sound Rose had made all morning. She was far enough back that no one else seemed to notice her outburst.

"That is very kind of you to say, Bill," I said.

Tommy shifted his enormous weight from one foot to another. I could tell he so badly wanted to add Bill's moniker but did not want to risk another backhand from Miss Cutty.

"Maybe we can take a look, Boss?" Luther said. "What'cha think?"

"I surmise there is no harm in that," I said. "After we have discussed a possible payment, of course."

"How's $5,000 sound?" Tommy said.

"And it looks as if my day has just opened right up," I said.

"Throw in that biscuit, maybe?" Luther said.

Tommy eyed Luther but did not respond.

"May I ask what most recently has gone amiss?" I said.

"I'm sorry to have to break the news like this, but it was a horse," Miss Cutty said, then looked to Bill, "It was... You know."

"Not Sugar!" Bill said, his head drooped and he had a look of sadness in his eyes.

No one consoled him.

ELIJAH'S ELIXIR

In the distance, a hare watched the lot of us trudge through the field, as we did our best to keep out of the cow flops that enveloped the area. The sun had finally managed to climb off the horizon and start its journey toward the west from which we had rode in. As the temperature rose, so did the smell of those prizes left behind.

Tommy and Miss Cutty had taken to either side of myself and told me what they knew, or more accurately, what they did not know. Between Tommy's size and Miss Cutty's limp, we did not move with a lot of hurry.

Luther and Bill lumbered behind. As expected, Rose offered to stable our horses and tuck our wagons away in Miss Cutty's barn, something she normally would not do, but a safe way to miss this trek through cow pie pasture.

"Used to be more cows here that belonged to Jim Brown," Tommy said as he attempted to step over a fresh cow pie, though he did not have the gait wide enough which caused him to step on first one side of the mess, and then the other. "Well, I guess what's left still are his, if he were to ever turn up. Though I'm feeling a little less optimistic about that with every day."

"Don't you say those things," Miss Cutty said. "I don't believe the powers that be would let anything happen to Jim. He was . . . is a good man."

"Be that as it may, when he didn't show up to the pecan pie festival, I took that as a sign," Tommy said. "No one misses that. Miss Cutty makes a hell of a pie."

"We all know something happened to you if you miss a meal!" Bill shouted.

Tommy turned and gave Bill a look, but caught eyes with Miss Cutty who he knew would not allow him to retort in the way he preferred.

I was not sure what the answer might be, but I was curious the standards needed to satisfy well enough to collect the $5,000. That was new wagon money. Hell, that was new start money. I just had to play it right.

Tommy noticed my silence.

"Well, sir," Tommy said. "Any guesses?"

"Elijah is fine," I said.

I scratched my chin to look inquisitive.

"Horses, a couple dozen cattle, the former Sheriff Boyd, and a possible Mr. Brown," I said.

"Few other folk," Tommy said.

Miss Cutty turned away.

"Also, one of Miss Cutty's boys," Tommy said with hesitation.

Miss Cutty took a few steps away. I could not see her expression but I could see her wring out the frilly edges of her apron in tight fists. A fresh wound, not that it would ever completely heal. It made me feel a little less happy about some of my financial considerations.

"Her younger boy, Joseph," Tommy said. "He vanished shortly after the sheriff. And that was before we realized something might be happen'n, so we thought maybe he'd just went somewhere without telling. But the more time passes, and the more people vanish. Well, again, not optimistic."

"You'd been in town not too long before," Little Bill said, as he and Luther caught up. "Smartest man I'd ever met, so I wanted to find you. See if you could help."

There legitimately was a mystery here. I looked around for some answer. The hare had gone about his way, and other than a few grazing cattle, there was not much of note.

"And no one has seen anything?" I said. "Heard anything?"

"Just Mr. Brown," Miss Cutty said. "Just said they would vanish. It was there, then it wasn't."

A smoke-filled, glassy stone caught my attention, sat atop a cow pie. I knelt down to get a closer look. Luther and Little Bill also leaned in.

"What ya see, Boss?" Luther said.

"Mineral deposit here," I said. "I have come across one like it before. Though seeing one here is quite unexpected."

My senses were assaulted with a smell best described as the sweet smell before a rain mixed with hot metal. The wind ripped across the field with a soft moan, strong enough Luther was holding his straw hat tightly on his head.

I turned to find the rotund sheriff. "What happened to Tommy?"

Everyone spun around in place, but there was no Tommy.

"Where'd he go?" Luther said. "He was right here."

A high-pitched scream caused me to look toward Miss Cutty, but she was still. It had been Little Bill, who looked on the verge of letting another one fly.

Luther walked over to where he had last been seen, as if he half expected Tommy to spring out from the soil.

"He ain't exactly a man you just overlook," Luther said.

The remaining four of us instinctively turned our backs toward each other and bunched up.

I twisted first one way, then the other, looking for answers. Any sadness on Miss Cutty's face from before had been replaced with fear. Luther's hands were in tight fists, ready to fight, but unsure of a target.

A lump in my throat got hard to swallow, like a bullfrog in my gullet had seen his moment to escape before it finally settled lower and hung in my stomach.

"I didn't see nothing," Bill said.

"Nor did I, Little Bill," I said. "But I do believe it would be in our best interest to . . . " and pointed toward the way we came.

"And that was it?" Rose said. "Gone, just like that?"

"Gone, just like that," I said.

I finished off my whiskey and spun the empty glass between my fingers. It burned a bit as it made its way down.

"He was there," I said, then cupped the glass out of sight. "Then he was not."

Rose knocked back her own glass and slammed it down.

"What about the $5,000?" Rose said. "That still on the table?"

We were close to alone in the Golden Eagle Saloon. Some had left town when the disappearances started, and the ones that were still here chose to stay out of sight.

"I will have to be honest with you Rose," I said. "I have my concerns that $5,000 might not be enough to keep me here."

"Oh bullshit," Rose said.

"I have had quite enough of that for the day," I said. "I was fine helping them look for an answer, but that was before I witnessed the occurrence within spitting distance."

"You'll walk away from a lot of things," she said, "but that amount of money ain't one of them."

"You did put the cart out of sight?" I said.

She gave me a look, disappointed I would even consider she might have made a misstep.

"Last time we were here, someone helped themselves to one of my kegs," I said. "Just being extra careful, as there is not much of it left. Though these days, Luther seems to be the one determined to lighten my load."

"Well, you have him sure that stuff is making him stronger," she said.

"Do not start this again," I said.

She was not pleased. Not allowing her to start things took away her favorite pastime.

"It does make people stronger," I said. "That is no falsehood. And you know why this is so important to me."

"Yes, yes," she said. "Your mother. Last wish. I've heard the story."

"I guess it would make sense to see if the money is still even a consideration," I said. "Soon as they pick out the new sheriff, I would reckon, though I do not know who would want the job."

"If the little horsefucker gets a vote, he'd pin that star on your chest himself," Rose said and showed me her empty glass, ready for me to remedy the situation.

"What did you really see?" I said. "In those cards with Bill."

Rose recoiled as if she had been asked to gargle sour milk. "What do you think I saw?"

"You could see that?"

"Wish the spirits had kept that one to themselves," she said.

"They have any insight to the question at hand here?" I said. "Where we misplaced a man bigger than the horses pulling our wagons?"

"You know they don't work like that," she said. "And don't bring up horses right now."

"Well, I agree with Little Bill on this one," I said. "That is very convenient."

The chair scooted along the wooden floor as I stood. Rose's mind seemed to wander. It is possible I had sent her back to some memories she had already tried to forget. I started toward the bar where we had left the bottle. Not exactly sure why I had not brought it to the table. Tradition, perhaps, as Bill had informed us even the bartender had skipped town.

As I leaned over the bar, I noticed a wiry man with a mustache tracking my every move. I grabbed the bottle and did my best to not convey concern. I watched from the corner of my eye to see if he would find other interests, but he was determined.

I quickly looked at him to see if he would drop his gaze, but he did not. Did not look away, or even offer a nod. I was the outsider here, so I decided to offer one of my own, and reached up to touch the rim of my hat, but then remembered I had left it in the wagon.

There was an awkward pause as I waited for him to react. He lifted one hand and smoothed the edges of his mustache.

"I've seen you before," the man said.

"What an exciting tale," Rose said, always the instigator. While no one held their liquor better than Rose, she was still capable of more hostility when she had a drink in her hand.

The man did not look her way. He was still fixed on me. Cards were spread in front of him where he had stopped a riveting game of solitaire to have this exchange.

"It is quite possible," I said.

"It's making me crazy I can't remember why I know ya," he said.

"Well, for something good, I hope," I said. "I was here some time back."

I thought it best to drop things and head back over to Rose. His gun hung from his hip, and I had not carried a piece in many years. I was an awful shot anyhow, so even if I had one, it likely would not have changed a thing.

I walked back over to my table with Rose and poured us both another shot. The man stayed fixated on me, and his game of solitaire remained unfinished.

"Let's just get the money, and go," Rose said.

"Who said anything about you getting any of it," I said, as I sat back down. "You better ask the spirits your chances of that happening."

"I already did," she said. "And they made a good point."

"That is rich," I said. "Please, enlighten me of this point your spirits made."

"Said you'd rather share the money," she said, "before you'd risk everyone leaving you here by yourself."

"Is that so?"

"That's so," she said, then looked over at the mustached man, raised her glass to him, and knocked it back. She slapped the empty glass down, let out a harsh breath, and started toward the door as her robes dragged the floor behind her.

"Make sure the money's still on the table," she said and pushed her way through the swinging doors that led outside.

I threw back my drink and felt it burn on the way down. "Damn spirits."

Miss Cutty had been kind enough to put us up in her home. She had a spare room she normally would rent for a little money, but with no travelers it was available. And with the disappearance of her son Joseph, there was an extra bed she could offer.

Her older son, Samuel, helped us bring in our things and showed us to our rooms. Rose was quick to claim the spare bedroom which left Luther and I to split Joseph's. Being Luther was the size of a grizzly bear and I was not much for cuddling, I knew I still needed to find somewhere else to lay my head.

There was some time before supper, and I decided to walk back into town. I balanced my hat on top of my head and started out. Miss Cutty's home was not too far. Far enough I would not have minded having a horse, but I had no real place to be and needed the time to think.

The path to town went right by Jim Brown's place. I had lost my nerve to examine the field, and now really taking note how close we stayed, it made me even more uncomfortable. I leaned on the fence that separated the field from the road. It was in need of repairs, but without Mr. Brown, and the fact the cows were unlikely to manage their own upkeep, it would just have to stay that way. I looked across the field, out where we had last seen Tommy. A cow, unaware of any reason to be concerned, stared back and chewed their cud. I could hear the wind as it ripped across the field with a soft moan.

I pushed away and started toward town. How could Tommy vanish like that? I had considered myself to be well-traveled with a good grip on how things functioned, but nothing made any sense. I weighed one idea, picked it apart until I knew it could not hold water, and started on another. The ideas got more and more outlandish until I was back in the main part of town, still without answers.

I came to the well near town and peered down. Not sure what I thought might be of interest, but it seemed like a thing to do. My hat slid forward and almost went in, but I caught it just in time. I should really have it sized, as the previous owner had a smaller head.

I turned around to find a young boy, wearing overalls and covered in a layer of filth. At first, I thought him to be a teenager, but saw he was a little younger with too much life already lived.

"You that magic man?" he said.

I thought a moment. "Because of the hat?" I said and balanced it back on top of my head.

"No, sir," he said. "Because of the 'lixer. Heard it can make people better."

"You heard correctly, Little Master," I said.

I peered back down the well.

"What do you think is down there?" I said.

"Water," he said.

"Well, that I figured," I said.

He shifted his feet around, not entertained by my inquiry.

"I was hope'n to try and buy some of that 'lixer from you," he said and pulled a few coins.

"Well, that is exactly why I have them," I said and pulled a bottle from my inside coat pocket. I looked at his handful of coins. "But, I am sad to say, I do not think you have quite enough there."

He fanned the coins out across his palm with the hopes that maybe I had missed some in my count.

"Not enough?" he said.

"I am sorry," I said.

"Is there anything I can do to maybe earn some coins from you," he said. "Or good favor?"

"Again, I am sorry, my young friend," I said.

He clutched his coins tight in his hand and stood there.

"I just need to save my maw," he said.

"Your maw?" I said and knelt down to his level.

"She can't get out of bed," he said. "Stopped eating. I just want to help her."

He turned to leave, and I reached out and grabbed his shoulder.

"I tell you what I will do for you," I said. "I am going to give you this bottle, but you have to do something for me in return."

"Anything, Mister," he said.

"Spend as much time with her as you can," I said and tucked the bottle into the pocket on his overalls.

Tears came to his eyes, and he thrust his handful of coins my way.

"That is not necessary," I said. "Just do as I said."

He took the bottle and yelled pleasantries as he went, but I was not able to make it out, as he was already halfway home.

I peered into the window of one of the shops. The last time I was here, I had purchased a jar of fresh marmalade, which I had managed to stretch out for almost a month. A man inside stocked the shelves, but there were no patrons. And from at least where I stood, no fresh marmalade. Previously, these streets were full. Wagons bounced up and down the road. Men and women pushed from store to store. The Golden Eagle previously surrounded by tough, hardened faces. All gone. That $5,000 started to feel smaller as I realized most people had smartly made the decision to hide or leave.

The wind whipped down the empty street, picked up dust and spun it around. I watched it dance toward the statue that stood in the middle of town and then settle down. That statue. I swear last time we were here, it still had both its limbs. I was curious if a name was mentioned and started toward it, but I had only taken a few steps when Little Bill emerged from between the buildings and spotted me. I noticed he had on a priest's robes, with the white collar and everything.

He waved like it had been ages since we had last seen each other. I waved back, not sure what else to do, and he picked up his pace. Like before, he talked the whole time he approached.

"Hey, Mr. Elijah," he said. "So, we talked it over and had sort of an emergency election to pick out a new sheriff. We had some concerns that if we went too long without one, things could get worse. No need for anyone to vote. No one left in town wants the spot. I tried to suggest you, but they didn't know you well enough to feel comfortable with that."

I was glad, as I had no desire to pin a star on my chest or have to explain that to him.

"Why are you dressed like a priest, Little Bill?"

"Because I am a priest," he said.

I looked at him with some confusion.

"I don't wear the robes when I'm out traveling," he said.

"That was not the . . . " I decided to let it go. "So, you were saying about the new sheriff?"

"Only one person in town left willing to do it," Bill said, now next to me. "Boyd, the former sheriff before Tommy, his daughter. And we had to beg her."

"Sheriff Boyd it is," I said.

"Oh, no," Bill said. "She didn't like her father, and the name reminds her too much of him, so we just call her Rebecca."

"I see," I said. "Does Rebecca know if that $5,000 is still available?"

Little Bill looked into the sky as if the answer might be there. "You know, I didn't think to ask. But I can take you to meet her."

"I knew I'd seen you!" I recognized the voice immediately. It was my mustachioed friend from before.

I spotted him through one of the saloon's open windows, peeking out. He ducked away to push through the swinging doors and step out into the street. He covered ground fast and headed straight toward me.

Bill took several steps backwards as he was looking for a hole to fall in, or for God to call him home.

"I am glad to hear you remembered," I said. "Might you remind me of our previous encounter?"

He made it across the street and was now on the wooden walkway where I was. The boards creaked with each step.

"Sir, I apologize that I do—" was all I could manage before he embraced me, which knocked me back and sent my hat tumbling.

I lightly patted him on the back, not sure what else to do.

"You saved my daddy," he said. His voice cracked and wavered as he spoke.

He finally released me and took a step back. He wiped his eyes and resmoothed his mustache. Bill reappeared, my hat in hand, now that the danger had passed.

"I didn't recognize you before without the hat," he said, "Had a cough those fancy doctors couldn't fix. Said he wouldn't live longer than a week. But Daddy drank your elixir and it put him right back on his feet."

"I am enthralled to hear he is doing better."

"Better, hell," he said. "We worked the field together this morning. The man's stronger than I am, now."

"I am but a simple man, selling my wares for enough to sustain me in my travels," I said.

"He's going to help us save Shadybrook," Little Bill said.

The man stuck out his hand, though it felt a little redundant following his embrace, but I shook it.

"Thank you, sir," he said and turned to leave.

He looked back over his shoulder as he stepped off the walkway. "Bless you for your kindness."

Bill and I were frozen outside the sheriff's office.

"I'm gonna kill you, you sonuva bitch!"

"She's in there," Bill said and pointed toward the screams coming from inside.

A loud crash punctuated one of her yells. I looked back toward Bill.

"She's still a little upset about before," Bill said. "Sheriff Tommy had her locked up for upsetting the peace. Part of the deal of her agreeing to be sheriff was we'd let her out."

"Upsetting the peace?"

"She cut the arm off the statue in town," Bill said.

"I was thinking that statue had both arms last time," I said. "Why did she do that?"

"Statue of her father," Bill said. "Like I said, she didn't like him much."

"I told you I'd kill every single one of ya!" the shouts continued.

I took a couple steps forward and looked back at Bill who was staying put.

"Little Bill, are you coming?"

"I'm sorry Mr. Elijah," Bill said. "Rebecca said I go back in there, she'll shoot me dead."

A chair thrown through the office window startled us both, and we spun around in time to see it hit the street and roll a few feet before it came to a standstill.

What was left of the window was replaced with the silhouette of a woman. Long black hair stuck out from under a leather cap. Her arm extended out the window, revolver in hand. She fired three shots into the chair, it jumped with each connection, she considered a fourth before she spun around out of sight.

Two more shots could be heard, in addition to the sound of her cursing.

"I'm not going in there, Mr. Elijah," Bill said. "I'll find you later."

And with that, Bill was gone.

I turned toward the office. It had gone quiet.

I took in a breath. "Five. Thousand. Dollars," I said to myself.

I stood outside the door, weighed my options, and settled on knocking.

A moment passed. I knocked again.

"Who the hell is it?" Rebecca yelled from inside.

"Elijah," I said. "The Elijah's Elixir, Elijah. Little Bill might have told you about—"

The door flew open, slammed against my shoulder, and knocked me to the ground.

I looked up to see straight down the business end of Rebecca's revolver. Her right shirt sleeve was rolled up and tucked upon itself, as I realized she was missing the arm to fill it.

"I should just shoot you right now and be done," she said.

She held the revolver on me another moment, then uncocked the hammer and went back inside.

I watched the door shut behind her, and then, silence. The absence of her screams unsettled me even more.

I got to my feet and picked up my hat, but held it as I went back to the door. Again, I knocked, only this time, left enough room for it to swing open. But it did not.

I pulled the door open a crack and glanced around the office. A desk covered in papers, a few rats shot dead, broken glass scattered around the floor, and Rebecca on a cot in the cells at the far end of the room. Her single arm thrown across her face, the revolver still gripped in her hand.

I was standing outside, not quite ready to step in.

"Sheriff Rebecca?" I opened the door the rest of the way. "They brought me here to help find out what is happening with—"

"I know why you're here," she said. "We don't have any money."

I took a step inside and shut the door behind me.

She raised her arm enough to peek out from under it.

"You hear what I said, Conman?" she said. "We got no money in this town."

I took another step closer, and then another, until I had made it to the desk. I sat on the corner, seeing as how the chair was gone.

"Why are you still here?" she said. "What part of what I'm saying is leading you to believe we still have business to discuss."

"Honestly, I am not sure," I said. "I was here because Sheriff Tommy—"

"That fat asshole," she said.

"That would be him, yes," I said. "He mentioned $5,000 . . . "

"And there it is," she said, and jumped up from her cot and stood in the doorway of the cell. She waved the revolver around the room. "You see any money around here?"

"Around here? No. I see some dead rats."

"I told those little bitey bastards I would kill them the moment they let me out," she said. "Unlike you, Conman, I am a woman of my word."

I looked toward the broken window. "Chair looked at you funny as well?"

She walked over and looked out the window.

"I didn't like that chair," she said. "Was Dad's, and he liked it, so it needed to die."

She fired another shot out the window, and I heard it hit. She had not missed yet.

"When are you going to ask me?" she said.

"Ask you?"

She turned around.

"Same thing every single person asks when they meet me."

She used the gun barrel to repeatedly flip the rolled-up part of her sleeve.

"The name of your tailor?"

"You must think you're funny."

"I have been known to tell a joke or two," I said. "But I will understand if you decide to hold your applause."

Her eyes met mine. Where was that line? Had I crossed it?

A laugh rolled out of her that reminded me of a donkey being beaten.

She gathered herself but her grin remained.

"Look here Conman," she said. "I meant what I said about there being no money."

I nodded my head.

"And soon as I say that," she said, "I know you're ready to pack up and move on."

I nodded, again.

"That is not to say I do not wish you and the people here of Shadybrook good health," I said, "But I am only a salesman. Not a lawman, or a scientist. And while the money was enough to make me curious, there is no real reason to stay without it."

This time, it was Rebecca's turn to nod. "First honest thing you've said."

Since we had returned from the field, Miss Cutty had been working in the kitchen. The entire house smelled delicious, and she had been kind enough to offer us all the meal. She mentioned cooking would take her mind off things, and she found herself doing it a lot since Joseph's disappearance.

I felt for her, but I was quite excited to have a real home-cooked meal. I tried to think back to the last time I had and realized it would have been from my own mother, years ago. I thought about the times I was in the kitchen with her in my youth. She was kind enough to call what I did, "helping," but honestly it was anything but. She never minded, though.

Reality crept in and thoughts of Mother became painful, so I pushed them all aside.

I stepped out onto the porch to get some fresh air and found Rose sitting outside, wrapped in her robes. We both looked across the field, our eyes drawn toward Jim Brown's cows in the distance.

"No money?"

"No money," I said.

She stayed silent.

"Spirits tell you?"

"Your face did," she said.

"You know what else? Bill is a priest."

"No," Rose said. "You can't be serious."

"Serious," I said. "And the new sheriff only has one arm."

Rose thought a moment.

"How does he reload?"

"She." I thought back to our encounter. "I am not really sure. Carefully, I would imagine."

"What's next?" she said.

"Was thinking we would eat supper," I said.

"I mean after that."

"Back to the road, I suspect. Maybe expand the route a little. Get a little more mileage from Luther."

Rose did not respond. The sun had finally gotten to the end of its journey and was beginning to melt behind the horizon where it leaked pinks and purples across the sky like spilled paint on blue canvas.

We had been on the road so long, I could not remember the last time I had actually stopped to appreciate the beauty of something as simple as a sunset. And while I did not have any spirits to tell me so, I believe Rose felt it, too.

The wind kicked up with a faint moan, turned almost musical, and drifted across the yard.

"Supper's ready," Miss Cutty said.

I was not sure when she had joined us, but the suddenness of her arrival caused me to jump a bit when she spoke. I turned to respond, but she was looking at Rose.

"All those blankets," she said. "You need to put on something a little more sensible for the supper table."

"I like my robes," Rose said.

"That may be, but if you're going to eat with us, I have some of my things for you to change into," Miss Cutty said. "I already laid a dress out in your room."

Rose started to respond but looked over to me shaking my head. The last thing we needed was to be put out, and I would never forgive Rose if I missed this meal.

Miss Cutty went back in and left me and a frustrated Rose to watch what was left of the day. Rose hemmed and hawed but did not say anything else. Then she went inside, I hoped, to change.

As hungry as I was, I lingered a bit as those pinks and purples grew darker, only to be replaced by pinholes of light across the night sky. This time, I did not push away the thoughts of my mother.

I was certain the overalls Rose had on was not what Miss Cutty had laid out.

Rose sat next to me at the table, and I leaned in close, "Why?"

Rose pushed her thumbs out against the shoulder straps of the overalls. She stood, turned first one way, then the other, to show off her outfit.

"Looks good, right?" she said.

Miss Cutty came from the kitchen with a bowl of mashed potatoes and noticed Rose's outfit. She slowed but continued on.

"Haven't seen those in quite some time," she said. "Abe, my husband, wore those to our wedding."

I stared hard at Rose, doing the best I could to ignite her head with my mind. She stuck her hands in the pockets and stretched them out to accentuate them like a butterfly's wings.

"I like how big the pockets are," she said and spun.

I looked to Miss Cutty, who watched Rose spin around and flap her arms like a baby bird, still not sure how to fly. This was it. Out on the street, only able to smell the food but never taste it. Thank you, Rose.

"Abe had wonderful taste," Rose said and gave a spin. "In clothes and women."

"They actually fit you quite well," Miss Cutty said with a bit of a laugh. "You're sort of built like a man."

Some of the wind went out of Rose's sails. She flapped a little less and sat down. Miss Cutty sat the potatoes down on the table and limped back into the kitchen.

Luther had on one of his nicer outfits, which meant the one with the least amount of stains, and leaned against the back of a chair as he watched me take a scoop of potatoes.

"Don't you think we should wait on Miss Cutty and the boy, Boss?" Luther said.

"I just want to try some of this food before Rose gets us thrown out," I said.

"She said I looked good!" Rose said and punched me in the arm.

I stuck a mouthful of potatoes in my mouth and chewed with exaggeration, smacking my lips in Rose's direction.

Luther pulled the chair out and took his seat. It creaked and groaned under his weight but held.

"Well, I'm going to wait," he said and crossed his arms. "I have a little thing called manners."

"Me, too," Rose said, and crossed her arms the same way.

"Where are your robes?" Luther said.

"I've been informed they are not sensible," Rose said, motioning toward the kitchen.

"Well, now you look like a man," Luther said.

"Keep hearing that, too," Rose said.

We all looked for someone else to carry the conversation, but none of us seemed to have anything to say.

"Miss Cutty?" Luther yelled out. "You want some help in there?"

No answer.

"Miss Cutty?" Luther asked with some caution.

He rose from his seat and stared toward the kitchen.

We waited for a sound. Any sound.

Luther took a few steps toward the kitchen door and balled up his fists. I stood up, though I was not sure yet if it was to help check the kitchen, or to charge out the door.

"Ma'am?" Luther said, meekly.

The door swung open and Miss Cutty came out with a dish in her hands with some sort of meat in it, completely unaware.

"You all have a seat," she said. "Samuel is bringing in some milk, for those that want."

The three of us collectively let out a deep breath, as we tried to remember how to breathe normally.

Luther went out and helped Samuel bring in the milk, then helped Miss Cutty bring everything out, including an entire tray of biscuits. I noticed he sat them near his spot at the table, and he looked at me with a grin.

The meal was as good as expected. And we even ended it with the aforementioned pecan pie. Tommy was right, it would take something quite devastating to cause a person to miss it.

"Really great pie," Rose said.

"I'll be sure to send some with you when you go," Miss Cutty said.

"You think you could also send some of these biscuits?" Luther said.

"I'm sure I can whip up another quick batch. I hate you're not staying," she said and looked to me.

"As I mentioned before, despite how Little Bill felt about me, I am no scientist," I said. "And while the idea of that much money got the better of me momentarily, Tommy turning to air put a bit of a spook in my head that I cannot shake."

Miss Cutty did not respond but instead finished off her slice of pie.

"Why not pack up and make your home somewhere else?" Luther said.

"Mama doesn't want to go anywhere else," Samuel said.

Miss Cutty reached under the table, and while I could not see from where I was, I knew she was twisting the ends of her apron in her fists.

"She wants to be here," he said, "for when Joseph comes back."

"Maybe Rose can help," Luther said. "She can see things. Tells people they're going to be rich or the future."

Rose looked at Luther as if he had spit in her face.

"See things?" Samuel said. "Like what kind of things?"

Luther did not continue, as he realized he had said too much. Everyone looked to Rose.

"I can't promise anything," Rose said. "The spirits tell me what they want to tell me. And they hate being put on the spot more than anything." Rose stared daggers at Luther as she spoke.

"Things about Joseph?" Samuel said. "Is that something you can try? Just to see what they say?"

Rose looked at Samuel, then to Miss Cutty, then to me. I was not sure why me, as she never listened to anything I ever said, or agreed to any suggestion I made. Perhaps for me to have an opinion so she could do the exact opposite.

"Maybe just give it a try?" Luther said and looked my way as if I had any say in the matter. "Don't ya think, Boss?"

I had learned long ago not to suggest Rose do anything and put my hands up in resignation.

"Please?" Samuel said.

Rose's shoulders dropped and she threw her head back in submission.

She sat up and looked at Miss Cutty and Samuel. "Do understand, I cannot promise anything. I cannot even promise you'll like the answer if we get one."

Rose continued talking at a volume I could not hear as she left the room and returned draped in her robes, her cards in hand.

She sat at the end of the table and pushed the dishes to make space.

The cards fluttered and popped as she shuffled.

"We shall see what the spirits say," Rose said. "Also, the spirits love coins, as a reminder. Just the toll for the soul."

No one moved as she shuffled again.

"We'll just call that pie payment," she said and focused.

"Spirits," she started. "We call, to those who fall. Reach out, and bring your message back to us."

She cut the deck and pulled a few cards from the top. THE EMPRESS. THE MAGICIAN. JUSTICE.

Rose laid her hands on top of the cards and closed her eyes.

Her voice changed. She spoke slower, and each word felt carefully chosen.

"Hot," she said.

Everyone exchanged glances.

"Burning," she said.

Miss Cutty reached to cover her mouth as a gasp escaped.

"Something else, Rose," I suggested.

"Something, else," she said. "Not, Joseph."

"Who is it?" Luther said. "Tommy?"

"No," she said. "Sophie."

Now she had my attention.

"Sophie?" I said.

"So, hot," Rose said. "Fever. Blood."

"Sophie who?" I insisted.

Rose took several deep breaths. Her fingers curled, the cards twisted up tight in her hands. Her face winced like she had been stuck with a hot poker. Her eyes peeled wide but only the whites looked back.

"Please, Rose," I said. "Sophie who?"

Samuel's face twisted up as he fought back tears.

Miss Cutty stood up, "No more. This isn't what—"

"STOP," Rose yelled out.

Everyone else did.

"Stop?" I said, on the verge of panic. "Stop what?"

Rose's eyes cleared and she looked intently at me.

"Everything."

The wagons were mostly packed. I did not blame Miss Cutty for asking us to leave. Samuel and herself were shaken from what happened, and I did my best to keep my own composure.

I carried a lantern as I went toward the barn.

Samuel was right behind me and stopped on the porch.

"Mama said there's no sense in sending you all into the night," he said. "She was just upset."

"Tell your mother we do appreciate her kindness, and her cooking," I said, "but we have overstayed our welcome."

Samuel did not respond.

"Have you seen Luther?" I said.

"He went to the barn," he said. "Had a cigar in his mouth. I was figger'n he went to smoke it."

"Thank you, boy," I said. "You take care of your mother. She is lucky to have you."

"I know," he said, and sat down on the edge of the porch, letting his legs dangle below. He kicked his feet out, letting his boots knock against the wood.

"And I do humbly apologize for the fright we gave you and—"

"I weren't scared, mister," Samuel said.

I nodded.

"Well," I said, "I apologize."

He continued to kick his feet but did not respond. I left him to make my way to the barn to find Luther. Rose's trunk was heavy, and I had found the best thing for my back was to have someone else do the heavy lifting. I liked to tell Luther my back was better from the elixir, but in truth, you cannot sell what you drink, so I let it heal up well enough on its own.

A crash from inside the barn caused me to take hurried steps.

"Luther, you best not be smoking around those kegs again," I said. "I told you before what happens when that stuff catches fire."

I swung the door open and held the lantern high to get a good look around.

One of my kegs was at the feet of Luther, busted on the ground.

"My God, Luther," I shouted. "What are you doing?"

"I can see them, Boss," Luther said. "I can see them."

I walked over to him and peered in the same direction, but nothing of note stood out.

"What are you on about?" I said. I turned back to look at his face. His eyes had turned smoke-filled, and gray-stained tears, as if from heated metal, streaked down his face and burned his cheeks.

"There's two close by," he said. "A big one, and a small one."

Luther looked right at me. "I can see them."

Luther stumbled toward the barn door and pushed his way outside. I followed behind a few steps. The smell from before, the hot metal mixed with rain, filled the air and assaulted my nose.

The moaning wind grew louder and started to sound like a siren in my ears.

"Luther," I said. "What is going on?"

"Boss, can you see me?" Luther said. "Can you hear me?"

"I am looking right at you, Luther," I yelled over the sound of the wind. "What is happening? What is wrong with your eyes?"

"The big one and the small one," he said. "They're pulling against each other. The small one wants to stop the big one but can't. It's not strong enough."

Samuel was still on the edge of the porch, but he was watching Luther stumble toward him.

"Mister?" Samuel said. "Are you okay?"

"Run!" Luther said. "Run, child!"

Samuel did not have to be told twice. He jumped up and ran inside.

"I have to help!" Luther said and reached out and grabbed at something that was not there, then pulled backwards until he was leaned at an angle that made no sense, yet stayed suspended in the air. He dug his boots into the ground and slid toward the porch.

Something was there, something big enough to pull Luther.

His heels drew deep lines as he pulled closer to the porch. His eyes were full of smoke. His muscles constricted as he tightened his grip and held.

I grabbed onto Luther's shirt, and it instantly ripped away. In desperation, I swung the lantern in front of Luther and hoped for it to find purchase, but nothing.

I swung again, harder this time, but still, nothing was there to hit. The momentum caused me to fall backwards and land in the dirt. I scrambled to my feet, but Luther was gone. The lines from his heels stretched several feet between the barn and the house and then stopped.

The smell dissipated, and the moans in the wind went dead.

I was still holding the ripped part of Luther's shirt.

"Luther?!" I said. "Luther!"

I looked around in desperation, but I already knew there would be no Luther to find.

Rebecca found me strapping things to the wagon. I threw my hat inside. I was done. My hands trembled any time I stopped, so I kept working. Kept busy. No time to think. No time to shake.

Samuel had run into town to fetch her, not sure what else he should do. For this town, Luther was just another name added to the list of missing people.

Rebecca picked up the lantern where I had left it and shined it first one way, then another. She walked around the area to see the whole lot of nothing. She held the lantern up high enough to illuminate me as I worked. Not to do me a favor, but to share her list of "I told you so's."

The flames from the lantern danced across the wagon and pushed away the darkness on my face.

"Did expect you to have more to say on the matter," Rebecca said. "Thought you'd already be finding a way to work this angle."

It was not like Luther and I were old friends, but I knew him. Had traveled with him. Shared meals with him. We did not go back as far as Rose and I, but . . .

Just get packed up. No more thoughts.

"Woke me up to look at the dirt," she said. "You have any idea how long it takes me to put on trousers with one arm?"

"You were right from the start, Rebecca," I said. "This is bigger than me, and for me to believe I was somehow smarter than everyone else . . . "

"Father Horsefucker told me about your mama," she said, "and you know what, I never believed a word of it."

My hands started to shake again.

"You got me," I said. "Just tell everyone to pack up and move. Whatever is happening here is going to keep happening. And it is going to take Miss Cutty, her other kid, you . . . "

"Sorry it took so long to get here," Little Bill said as he walked toward us. He donned his priestly robes. "No one would let me borrow their horse. Heard something happened to Luther."

"I told you I didn't want to see your face," she said.

Bill stopped his approach.

"This ain't your office!" Bill said.

"Who said anything about my office?" she said. "What you did to Sugar has nothing to do with my office."

Bill knew better than to try to plead his case.

"I forgive you of the darkness in your heart," Bill said and motioned toward Rebecca.

"And this is your hero?" Rebecca said and held the lantern up toward me.

"Wait," Little Bill said, and approached me, forgetting about Rebecca. "You're leaving? I thought you were going to help."

I strapped down Rose's trunk. Without Luther, I had been forced to drag it myself.

"Said we should all just pack up and leave," she said. "And the more I think on it, might be the smartest thing he ever said."

I leaped down from the wagon, grabbed the lantern from Rebecca, and started toward the house to find Rose. I just wanted to leave. Little Bill stepped forward and grabbed my shoulder forcefully enough to spin me toward him. His face was filled with desperation.

"Mr. Elijah, we need you," he said. "God himself told me you were the answer. Nobody else here is a scientist and—"

"I told you already Bill," I cut him off. "I am no scientist."

I took a deep breath, "I was a blacksmith. And not even a good one."

Bill stepped back to let that shift between his ears.

"Blacksmith?" he said. "But . . . The stories about the elixir."

"Stories," I said.

"There's that truth," Rebecca said. "Let him go, Horsefucker. Told you he made up all the stories about his mother, too."

"I did not lie about my mother," I said. "There are places I might have stretched the truth, but that was only in the spirit of the story."

"I don't . . . " Bill stammered. "I really don't understand. I spent so much time finding you . . . "

"Well, I do not know what to tell you about that," I said. "Maybe ask your God."

And I turned back to my mission to find Rose.

Little Bill took a few steps in my direction before his attention shifted to something near his feet.

"Mr. Elijah," Bill said and held up a stone. "Was the part about knowing what these funny look'n rocks are, also not true?"

I twisted back to see, holding the light toward the object he held in his hands. It was a smoke-filled, glassy stone, like the one we had found in the field. Like the ones I knew very well.

Rebecca stepped forward and snatched it from Bill and held it up toward the light.

"Let me have it," I said.

I reached for it, but she spun fast and hit me with her elbow right in the throat. Before I had even found my footing, she had jammed the stone in her pocket and pulled her revolver and pointed the loud end my way.

But that was the least of my concerns, as I was still trying to negotiate the situation that had started with my lungs, bent over with my hands on my knees.

"Don't think for one moment that I'm a pushover," she said. "If there was two of you, I can whip both your asses with my one arm tied behind my back. And if you're not sure, I invite you to find out."

I tried to take a breath, but nothing.

"Time to get an honest streak about you," Rebecca said. "This isn't the first one of these I've seen, either."

That was not expected. Rebecca holstered her gun and pulled the stone back from her pocket.

When I finally was able to take a breath, I answered.

"It is what goes in the Elixir." The words hung like thick fog.

I feared for a moment Rebecca might hit me again.

"What I said about my mother was true," I said. "She was sick. Last days, sick. And this guy bumps into town with his wagon, picture of him wearing that top hat painted on the side. Says he has this magic elixir. I was desperate and he was offering me her cure, but it cost me everything. But it worked. Mom was back on her feet in a couple days. Cooking and singing in the kitchen like she used to. She used to sing this song about a frog named Lumps that went on an adventure. No idea where she heard it from."

"I thought you said she died," Rebecca said.

"Elixir worked," I said. "For a while. But whatever was rotten inside her before, it came back. Worse than before."

I realized I had been pacing as I talked about Mom and found myself near the porch. Bill and Rebecca had followed. I took a seat on one of the steps of the porch as I considered my words.

"And again, I was desperate," I said. "Went looking for the man in the top hat. I needed more. I needed to know how it was made. But he was not talking. I had nothing left to sell. But I was going to help my mother. And when I was done, he told me about these stones, and about melting them to make the elixir. Not that he wanted to tell me, but I was . . . persuasive.”

“You killed him?” Bill asked.

“I did not,” I said. “I left him a little worse than I had found him, but I did not kill him. Took his hat and all of the elixir I could find, and all was right in my world. Mom was back to singing about that frog every morning. But I am guessing you know where this ends up.”

“No more Lumps,” Bill said.

“No more Lumps,” I said. “I feared she had fallen ill again. Maybe had forgotten to take the elixir, but no. The only thing I found in her bed was one of these stones.”

I had more to say, but no words to say it. The shake in my hands returned.

“I don’t understand,” Bill said.

Rebecca turned the stone over.

“I don’t believe it,” she said. “If this really does make people better and stronger, then why aren’t you taking it?”

“What sounds better? Strong, or rich?”

“You think this is Luther?” she said.

“I am not sure what I think,” I said.

“Can I see it?” Bill said.

Rebecca looked at him, and he took a couple protective steps away, worried she might lay into him. I believed it to be a worthwhile concern. She tossed the stone toward him.

He panicked, juggled it a little as he caught it, and he pulled it tight against him.

“Be careful!” he said. “If this is Luther, I don’t want him to break.”

“You found a stone, also?” I said.

Rebecca sat down next to me.

“I found one the day my dad vanished,” she said. “One of the best days of my life. He had always been a mean bastard. He didn’t like me running around with some of the boys in town, so to make his point he had strapped my arm to Sugar, saying I was gonna stay tied there while we plowed the field ‘til I learned the meaning of hard work.”

She reached up and flicked the folded sleeve of her missing arm.

“Old bastard thought it’d be funnier to fire his gun to make

Sugar take off running. Drug me all around that field, hopped the fence, and straight into town. Whole time, I could hear Dad just a hooting and laughing. Funniest thing he ever saw, he'd tell people, my body flopping this way and that, me trying to get my footing only to get pulled back down. People said they could hear the screams all the way into town."

Rebecca and I sat in silence all while Bill kept looking at the stone.

"So, why would your father and my dying mother have both turned to stones?" I said.

"I know he stole one of the kegs from your cart last time you were in town," she said. "Heard you say it made people stronger. He didn't know if you were telling the truth, but he just didn't want to pay."

All this time, I had believed the original man in the top hat had come back for revenge, maybe took my mother, left the stone as a message.

"Did I kill my own mother?" I finally said out loud.

"Maybe," she said. "But maybe you gave her more time."

"You didn't kill your mom," Bill said, holding the stone up to his ear.

"That is kind of you to say."

"No, I'm serious," he said. "Whatever is happening, Sugar didn't drink that elixir. Or all of Jim Brown's cows."

The wind picked up, strong enough to cause Rebecca to shield her face with her hand as she spoke.

"The Horsefucker has a point," Rebecca said.

"And there's something else," Bill said, still holding the stone to his ear, and started to sing.

" . . . and Lumps packed all his bags, and then off he went," he sang. "Without even a care, and without even a cent."

My mouth went dry. "How do you know that?"

"I can hear her," Bill said, with the stone against his ear. "I can hear her sing."

"So, when you swim, do you go in circles?" Rose asked Rebecca.

"Why are you dressed like a bed?" Rebecca said.

Miss Cutty stepped forward. "Both of you stop," she said. "We don't have time to talk about Rose's bad choices."

"Everyone," I said. "Listen to me. My mother is alive. I had not really had time to process what had happened with Rose's reading, but Sophie who had tried to come through I am sure was my mother. I think she was trying to warn us. And maybe there's something we can do to save her and bring her back."

"Save her from what?" Miss Cutty said. "Is Joseph alive, too?"

"That I do not know," I said. "It is something to do with the elixir, but I do not understand how people not exposed to it, like Joseph, also vanished."

"If we could talk through the reading, maybe Rose can do another?" Bill said. "Try to reach out to—"

"Why is he here?" Rose said, pointing toward Bill. "No part of me wants to see his face."

"That's something we can agree on," Rebecca said.

"Rose, please," I said. "It is something we could try."

I hated asking her.

Miss Cutty spotted Samuel peeking out from his bedroom and she went to put him back to bed. I was glad, as I did not want her to be present if it was anything like a repeat of before."

"And the last time, that did not work so well," Rose said.

"I know," I said. "But I do not know what else to do."

Rose took a deep breath as she made her familiar face of frustration.

"Everyone take a seat. We're going to all find out the hard way," she said. "I honestly do not know what will happen."

We took our seats and Little Bill reached his hands out.

"This isn't a séance, Horsefucker," Rebecca said. "And I'm not touching your hand. I can't risk the one I have left."

"Jesus believes in forgiveness," he said.

"Well, he's nicer than I am," she said.

Rose pulled her cards from her robes and started to shuffle them. They popped and clapped as she shuffled them over and over. We watched as she got ready to pull the cards, and froze, and just stayed that way.

"Rose?"

"Don't see Rose," Rose said in a voice that was not hers. "Just me here, Boss."

"Luther!" Bill shouted excitedly.

"Is that you, Little Bill?" the voice said.

"Luther, can you understand me?" I asked.

"Something happened to me," the voice said. "I don't know where I am. I'm there, but I'm also not there. Like I'm floating."

"Luther," I started. "Do you still see the two creatures? The ones you told me about?"

"Creatures?" the voice asked. "Yes, the creatures. I see hundreds. They're here . . . But they're also not here."

"Alright," Rebecca said. "Enough of this. What is going on? What do you see?"

"The world that was, I am now beyond it," the voice said.

"That doesn't mean anything," Rebecca said.

"To a fish, the river is the whole world," the voice said. "I am no longer in your river, I have crawled onto the shores of another world, looking back only to see how small everything from before was. There is so much more."

"It sounds like the stories of Heaven," Bill said. "Is that where you are?"

"Perhaps," the voice said. "But no. There are others here, dipping their toes into the world we used to share. Time seems to be different here. I've walked the shores of this life for lifetimes now."

"You've only been gone a few hours," Bill said.

"And my mother," I said. "Is my mother there?"

"I don't know your mother," the voice said. "But I do know one of the creatures comes here to feed. The one that pulled me through, and also a woman who tries to stop him."

"The woman," I said. "What does she look like."

"Shadow, darkness, something made of nothing," he said. "I only know she was a woman because I could hear her when she sings."

"What do you mean by feed," Rebecca said.

"Is there a way to bring my mother back?" I said.

"You back as well, Luther," Bill said.

"The other shape here," the voice said. "The Greedy One. He pulls the life from your world."

"Maybe you can tell us how to get you out," I said. "How to get Mom back. We could get you both back and get you more of Miss Cutty's biscuits."

Even inside, the wind picked up and knocked the plates off the table as the smell from before grew stronger. A biscuit from the plate hung in the air a moment, then popped out of view.

The wind died down.

"I missed them, Boss," the voice said. "But they will not exist in this world. They crumble away. Only what has life can be pulled in to be absorbed."

"Absorbed?" Rebecca said. "What does that even mean?"

"Life here is like water," he said. "If you pour a bucket of water into the ocean, the water still exists, but it is now part of the ocean. The Greedy One wants to grow. I believe the elixir let me cross on my own. But the only other way here is being pulled through from this side to become a part of this world, a power The Greedy One siphons for himself."

"How do we stop him?" I said. "How do I get my mother back? Does that mean my mother is like you? Not absorbed?"

The voice did not respond, and Rose started to shake. She fell to the floor and convulsed.

Little Bill let one of his screams fly and fell backwards.

"Stop screaming!" Rebecca yelled.

I felt helpless as Rose thrashed around.

"Can we not do something?" I asked Rebecca.

"I look like a doctor?" she said.

She leaned down close to Rose who was still shaking and slapped her across the face.

"What are you doing?!" I yelled.

Rose's body stopped seizing. She let out a groan and opened her eyes.

"Why does my face hurt?"

Bill was back on his feet and reached down to help Rose, but she slapped his hand away.

"Don't touch me," Rose said. "As a matter of fact, go stand in the corner."

Bill did.

"And turn around," she said.

And again, he did.

She was still having trouble standing in the robes. She rolled around like a turtle on its back. Rebecca reached down and pulled.

"You're gonna have to do some of the work," Rebecca said. "I only got the one."

They went back and forth, eventually pulling Rebecca down as well. Rebecca rolled to the side, made like a tripod, and jumped to her feet.

"Those robes are just not sensible," Rebecca said.

"I've been hearing that," Rose looked to me. "You could help, you know."

I grabbed one of her arms, Rebecca grabbed the other, and we pulled Rose to her feet. Rose brushed herself off and rubbed the side of her face where Rebecca had slapped her.

I wondered, was it possible to save them? To pull them back into our river?

"Can I turn back around, yet?" Bill said.

"No," Rose said.

He did anyway, with the stone against his ear.

"But I think you should hear this," he said and extended the stone.

I reached out before I realized he was handing it to Rebecca. She held it against her ear.

"What is it?" I said. "Luther? My mom?"

"Someone else," Bill said.

Rebecca's face sank.

"It sounded like a laugh," he said. "Sort of like a distressed donkey."

"That son of a bitch," Rebecca said. "It's my father."

"The Greedy One," Bill said.

The shakes returned.

"I cannot think with everyone yelling," I said and gripped my hands together in hopes they would steady. "I thought I was helping."

"You thought you'd make a quick buck," Rebecca said.

It was hard to argue. She was right.

Miss Cutty pulled out the chair across from me and sat down. She reached out and squeezed my hands.

"I know you're hurting," she said. "But I want you to know, I will never forgive you for what happened to my boy."

She squeezed as hard as she could as she spoke.

Bill let out a gasp as he stepped forward. "You don't mean that, Mildred."

"I do," she said. "With every ounce of pain I've felt every night since he went missing."

"Do not forget what the Bible says about—" Bill started.

"Don't give me that Bible business right now," she said, and dropped her grip and turned toward him. "You know that no one here loves the good Lord as much as I do, but the Lord also speaks of retribution against greed and wickedness."

Miss Cutty turned back toward me, "And he deserves every single thing I've said."

"Mildred—" he started.

"She is right," I said. "I deserve every bit of it."

Everyone was silent.

"I have to go after them," I said.

Rose stepped forward, "Go after them? What does that even mean? No part of me even thinks you deserve some punishment because I know you, and you wouldn't have done any of it had you known."

"Being ignorant of it does not excuse it," I said.

"Great, fine, whatever," Rose said. "What good is going after them? You think Luther wouldn't just come back if he could? Wherever he is, that is the unknown. And you have no way of knowing if her kid, or your mom, or Luther can even come back."

"You are right," I said.

"Well, if I'm right, listen to what I'm saying," she said.

"I am," I said. "And have already thought about every single thing you have said. But I can either do nothing, or do something, and I owe it to everyone to do something."

"You don't owe anyone, anything," Rose said.

I stood up and walked over. I noticed she had tears in her eyes.

"So," I said, "you do care."

"Shut up," she said and pushed me away.

"One of those stones produces several kegs worth," I said. "Heat turns it into the liquid, but it is thick and would be hard to drink it all at once, and I need this to happen now."

I went over to Rebecca and put out my hand. She hesitated, then reluctantly dropped it into my palm. I held it up, the gray and silver smoke inside swirled around and crashed over itself like fighting waves.

As I handed the stone to Miss Cutty, "Do you think you could bake it into a pie? It should expand some but I think that would work."

Miss Cutty took the stone and gave me a look. For a moment,

I thought maybe she might forgive me, but if she did, she kept it to herself.

"You're an idiot," Rebecca said. "You have no plan, no idea, no nothing."

"I know," I said.

"Cut me a slice of that pie," Rebecca said. "I'm coming, too."

"There is no reason that—" I started.

"I'm not looking for your reasoning, and after you just gave that big speech, I'm not looking for you to tell me why it's a bad idea," she said. "It's my father causing these problems, and he and I have unfinished business. And death settles all ill will."

I was glad to have her.

"Miss Cutty," I said. "Fire up that oven."

Worst case, I was going to have one final piece of pie before nothing happened. Now that I think on it, there were a lot of worst cases.

It sat on the table where we had eaten dinner not long ago. The sun was starting to peek in through the windows and I only noticed then how tired I was. Not that I could have slept. There is no way I could have quieted my mind with what could be my last meal, baking nearby.

At first, it looked just like the pecan pie from before, but the silver metal started to bubble and rise to the surface. And it was hot, yes, but there was no setting this one on the windowsill to cool, it was getting even hotter.

"Well," I said. "It is not going to eat itself."

Rebecca and I pulled up the chairs next to it, each of us with a fork in hand. Rose, Bill, and Miss Cutty gathered nearby, curious more than anything else.

"Here goes everything," I said and jammed my fork into it.

The force of the explosion caught me completely off guard. It threw Rebecca into Bill and Rose, and sent me the other way, knocking me against the far wall.

Then, everything reversed and pulled all of us toward where the pie had been, now replaced with a portal that was hungry for our world.

Rebecca grabbed at anything she could, finally getting a fist full of Rose's robes. Bill and Miss Cutty did the same, and all gripped the material. Rose held them all, her arms twisted around the door frame to the kitchen.

Chairs slid across the ground, leaped into the air, and flew into the beyond. Another did the same, but caught the side and it splintered like it had hit something hard.

I clawed at the ground, unable to find anything to grip. The hot metal from the pie leaked out and crawled across the table and dripped onto the floor below. Stronger than ever before, the smell of burning metal and rain invaded my senses. It was in every breath I took as I gasped harder and harder as I slid toward the pie hole.

Close enough to the table, I was able to brace myself with my legs against it. The hot metal crawled closer and inched toward my boots.

Then, it stopped.

It was at that moment I realized someone had been screaming, and while I looked to Bill, I discovered it had been me.

The room had settled but was still putrid with the smell, and the heat from the pie, and the portal remained.

We each stood, keeping our distance, not sure what would happen next.

Rebecca was on her feet, her revolver already pulled, inching closer and closer.

Then, we heard her.

"His travels took Lumps, from one shore to another," the voice said. "He missed all his kin, but mostly his mother . . . "

"Mom?" I said.

The voice did not return. Just silence.

I got to the table's edge, close to the portal, and hesitated. "Mom?" I said into it.

But no response.

I looked toward the others who were mixed between fear and curiosity.

I glanced around for something and saw the fork I had before. I lobbed it into the portal. It made a wet slurp noise as it passed inside, but otherwise, nothing else happened.

I stared inside, not sure what to do. Rebecca appeared at my side, her revolver still pointed into the silver and gray swirl.

I reached out and gently pushed the barrel down, fearing she might somehow endanger Mom.

Bill appeared on the other side. He had one of the broken chair's legs, and he extended it out like he was offering the portal a snack.

It did not seem interested. It slipped inside with another slurp noise, and he pulled it back out, unchanged.

Bill looked at the end that had made the journey with fascination, then got an odd look about himself.

He reached his hand out and stuck it inside and screamed. I grabbed him and pulled him away. We looked at his arm. Untouched.

"Why'd you scream?!" Rebecca said.

"Because it was cold," Bill said and rubbed his arm.

"Why are you such an idiot?" Rose yelled.

Samuel had come from his room and was mesmerized by the portal. He started to inch closer until Miss Cutty spotted him. She snatched him up and took several steps back.

"What do we do?" Miss Cutty said. "What do we do with it?"

"Back to the original plan," I said. "I just will not be able to enjoy your pie. Possibly ever again."

I looked toward Rose, her expression said it all. I turned to Rebecca and nodded. If she was coming, this was her invitation.

An arm burst from the portal. A giant's arm. The portal had grown large enough that I could squeeze through, but whatever was reaching out had to stop at its shoulder.

The arm itself was covered in burns mixed with that look of metal. It covered the length of it and stretched down to its long fingers.

It slapped around on the floor like it had dropped its eyeglasses behind the bed.

We all scattered and squeezed against the wall. Miss Cutty gripped Samuel and fled into his bedroom to safety.

The giant hand continued to bounce around, slamming its palm on the floor hard, each time with a deafening thud. We tried our best to stay out of reach. A few more thuds, until it found Bill. It gripped him tight, and I could hear Bill's insides being squeezed.

The donkey laugh from before echoed out from behind that massive shoulder and continued to smash Bill.

"Is that you, little Rebecca," the creature said between laughs. "Still just as worthless as before?"

Rebecca let her revolver respond and fired off all six rounds, each one hitting its enormous elbow. It yelped in pain, then tightened its grip.

"This one's not you," the voice yelled out as he crushed Bill even tighter. "No, no, this one still has both arms. I was hoping to hear you in pain, again. I always enjoyed that."

"Shoot him! Shoot The Greedy One!" Bill yelled as he gasped for breath.

"What do you think I'm doing?!" Rebecca said.

Rose leaped forward and grabbed onto the massive creature's wrist, and I joined on the other side, but as it flopped around, it threw us without even taking notice we were there.

"Get the spirits!" Bill said. "Tell them to help!"

Rose responded between thrashes, "They. Don't. Work. Like. That."

Rebecca flipped open the chamber, spilled the spent bullets, tucked the handle between her knees, and with one hand, slipped in new bullets from her pocket, all in a matter of seconds, faster than I could have done it with two hands and a lifetime of practice.

And just like that, her revolver had plenty to say again, all six shots found a new home from wrist to elbow of the creature. It yelped again and threw Bill upwards where he hit the roof. Rose and I, aboard for the ride, flew up and landed back down. Bill collapsed on the floor and did not move.

The arm pulled back and Rose and I were happy to let it go.

Rebecca was clicking a new set of bullets in as the arm slithered back out of sight and was replaced with a massive eye that looked out before it moved again to see a giant mouth that barfed the burning metal out toward her.

Rebecca jumped to the side, clicked the revolver closed, and emptied it into the portal. But the eye vanished and it was like before, just a dead space between the worlds. The wall beside her dripped with melting metal and burned into the wood.

Rebecca was already reloading.

Rose and I went over to Bill. His insides had been crushed, a rib poked out from his priestly garb, he leaked out of every hole he had, and some new ones he had been given. Bill was done for.

"Thought you said I'd die rich," he said to Rose between gasps and coughs.

"Sometimes the message doesn't resonate," she said. "It happens."

"That's pretty convenient," he said. "Maybe in the next life."

And with that, Bill was gone. The donkey laugh from inside the portal filled the room.

Rebecca stepped toward the portal and emptied her revolver into it, and while the laughing went quiet, I got the feeling it did not change anything.

It had been hours since the hand vanished back into the pie hole. Bill was laid outside, left with promises to bury him near Sugar's former pen.

Rebecca rarely took her eyes from the portal. She gripped her revolver, ready to feed it more lead.

"Do you think it . . . " Miss Cutty started, "Do you think it has my Joseph? Do you think he looks like that? All burnt up?"

None of us were sure who she was even asking. Not that it mattered. None of us knew more than she did. All we knew was The Greedy One had just turned Bill's insides into mashed potatoes.

"Bill was able to put his hand in," I said. "Back to the original plan, I am thinking."

"And do what exactly?" Rose said. "You can't shoot, you can't fight, and honestly, you're not much of a fast talker, despite selling this elixir."

"The elixir sold itself," I said. "I was a blacksmith! I got metal hot and hit it with a hammer."

"Well, isn't that just wonderful," Rose said. "Maybe you can find your big hammer."

"That's not a bad idea," Rebecca said. "The blacksmith in town was one of the people to go missing. We never were sure if he left town or was taken, but he left all his things behind."

"I'll get it!" We had not noticed that Samuel was once again listening from his room. He was out the door faster than any of us could stop him. Miss Cutty gave chase, but with her limp and his determination, there was no way she would catch him.

"I need to go in," I said. "I need to try to find Mom."

"Did you want to wait on the hammer?" Rose said.

"How do you think I wore out my back?" I said. "I had no plans of deceiving anyone. I lost Mom, I could no longer swing a hammer. I really believed this elixir was helping people, and it brought in enough money I thought I might never need to want for anything again. Rose, I know it is a stupid idea, but I have to go. I have to try to do something. I owe it to everyone."

"Well, Conman," Rebecca said, then reconsidered. "Elijah. I'm coming with you."

"You better come back," Rose said. "I like having you around."

I nodded, then Rebecca and I went in.

It was dark. Bottom of a cave up a crow's ass on a moonless night dark. There was no waiting for my eyes to adjust. It was nothingness, and it would stay that way. The smell of burning metal was stronger than even before, and without anything visual, my nose was working overtime. It was almost too strong to continue.

I wish I had brought the lantern. I felt around in the darkness.

"Rebecca, you here?" I said.

At least I thought I said it. Sound did not work the same here. Words I spoke sounded like they came from far away as if someone in the next room over had whispered them.

I tried to listen for Rebecca. For all I knew, she was standing right next to me. I waved my arms about, looking to make contact with her, or anything, but nothing. Just me flapping in the dark.

Then I heard a voice.

"Lumps went everywhere he could, always ready to roam," the voice sang, "until he could do it no longer, and turned back for home. The lily pad he left behind may have looked like all the rest, but after seeing them around the world, he knew it was the best."

"Mom?!" I ran blindly in the direction I heard her. "Please tell me where you are. Please."

Darkness had swallowed everything and running toward her voice only made her sound farther away. There were no walls to feel, nothing to orient myself. I knelt down and touched the ground, only it did not feel like wood or dirt. It flowed around my fingers and pulsated with a heartbeat. The more I felt it, the louder it got. Thump thump. Thump thump. Everything felt connected. Up was down, down was up. Everything was nothing, and black was . . . well, black was still black.

The donkey laugh echoed from every direction and I sprung to my feet. I tried to run away from the laugh but found no matter which way I went, it stayed just as loud. I finally collapsed on the floor, the heartbeat thumping against my face. I was lost. That was until Rebecca's hand took mine, and pulled me to my feet.

I tried to say something, but my voice was gone, lost in another world. No sound, except that damn laugh. It was everywhere, and unrelenting.

It felt like hours, being drug through the darkness. Unable to say anything, only that laugh able to exist. Did Rebecca know where we were going? It was my fear she was just as lost. Then a light. The first light I had seen in ages. It was the light of my river. And there in it stood a concerned Rose. She would have hated to know I could see how much she worried.

As I got close, a second hand grabbed onto mine. Wait, a second hand? This could not be Rebecca. Mom? I tried to stop, but they were too strong and pushed me back into my world.

I tripped as my feet hit familiar ground again. It was like I had sea legs. Rose rushed over and seemed to be looking at me from top to bottom, checking if I had come back with all the limbs I had left with.

Rebecca stepped in from outside, the lantern in her hand.

"I thought you were with me?" I said to her, finally finding my voice again.

"It was too dark," Rebecca said. "Couldn't see anything."

"You left me in there all this time?"

"You've only just went in," Rose said.

It had felt like hours, maybe even days.

"Mom!" I shouted, and jumped to my feet, remembering my guide in the darkness.

I shouted into the void. "Mom! Mom!"

"Did you find her?" Rose said.

"I think I did," I said. "Someone was in there with me. Someone with two hands."

"Wow," Rebecca said.

"Look, I did not mean—" I started, but heard the slurp of something passing through the portal, and another right behind it. I turned to find the giant burnt fingers from before gripping the portal, tearing it open with ease. Turning our small hole into something larger as it ripped down the seam of our worlds. He shrunk down to fit through the new entry. He was still triple my size, but smaller than when he had smashed Bill.

Rose sprinted for the door. I was not sure if Samuel had ever returned, or even had enough time to, but I was banking on that as not seeing him or Miss Cutty there meant they were safe for the moment.

I looked at Rebecca who had planted her feet. She had no plans of going anywhere. She swung the lantern to me, and as I caught it, her revolver started talking again. And it had plenty to say as it knocked holes in The Greedy One as he squeezed out into our world.

"I didn't think you could be a bigger asshole," Rebecca said. "But I guess you proved me wrong."

The donkey laugh from Boyd shook the house and he sprung upward, his head near the roof. Rebecca was already doing her knee-pinch reload, snapped it shut, and went to work emptying it his way.

Boyd swung toward Rebecca, but she was fast, and still plenty angry. Boyd would swing, and Rebecca would continue to feed him lead while he laughed. Then it happened. Rebecca had run out of room, and one of Boyd's swings made contact.

It knocked her to the ground and her gun skittered across the floor near me. Rebecca looked my way and reached out but Boyd was over her and brought his giant fists down on top of her.

She yelled out in pain. "Ahhh, my favorite sound," his voice boomed like thunder, existing as large as he did.

He brought down his fist again, but this time, no sound. He waited, then swung again. SMASH. But nothing.

"Disappointing," he boomed.

He reared back to give her another, jumped back surprised as another gunshot echoed out. It was only then I realized I had picked up the gun and shot.

The donkey laugh started up again, as bullets seemed to be more the annoyance of an ant's bite, than anything to turn the tide. It also did not help that most of the shots had completely missed. A target as big as he was, and I still somehow missed.

"I get to hear my favorite sound again," Boyd boomed. "It won't be as good, but you will do."

I pulled the trigger again, but it was empty. The only thing I had accomplished was to give away my position. At least he was no longer hitting Rebecca. I was not sure if she was still with us, but she had taken enough.

He reached for me, and I leaped to the side. "Why are you running little man? Let me crush you, too. You rattled the cage of your new god."

I made it to the front door and took inventory of what I had. Rebecca's empty gun and the lantern. I chunked the gun to the side as I hit the porch. Rose and Miss Cutty were both standing outside and they saw me booking it out of the house. Miss Cutty's body rocked in every direction, doing her best to really hustle, despite her limp. Rose grabbed her hand and pulled her down the road.

There was nowhere that seemed safe but far sounded like the right idea.

I turned back to see Boyd walking out behind me, and he threw back his head and laughed again.

I saw the barn, then it hit me. I knew right away it might not work, but it was the only idea I had, which made it the best idea there was.

Boyd started my way, his large lumbering legs covered ground faster than I could. I looked back, now able to see him clearly. The look of metal mixed with burn marks covered every inch of him. He stomped closer as I ran through the barn door.

Boyd snatched off the door of the barn and saw me next to the kegs of the elixir, one of them in my arms.

Boyd's hand reached, I thought for me, but he grabbed one of the kegs, and used his giant fingers to crush open a side, then turned it up to drink.

It spilled in and around his mouth, flowed across the scales on his burned skin, and dripped down onto the ground around him. I lobbed the keg I was holding his way and it shattered against him, spilling the elixir all around him. He stopped drinking long enough to laugh again. It was the best it was going to get.

I picked up the lantern and threw it at him. It shattered at his feet and the flame went up instantly into a giant blaze. The fire started at his legs and climbed across his entire body. As far as I could tell, he was made of the stuff, and as I had learned previously with Luther, it was insanely flammable.

The Greedy One no longer cared about me. He was a giant fireball with legs. He started to run, but that only fanned the flames. In his panic, he fell into the kegs and the eruption that followed sent the walls of the barn in every direction. Wooden shrapnel rained down from above.

It had thrown me toward Jim Brown's field, just short of the fence line. Miss Cutty and Rose rushed to where I had landed, but none of us could turn away from Boyd who was starting to move slower and slower. He stopped and yelled out in pain.

"You were right!" I yelled at him. "That is a satisfying sound!"

I was not sure if he had heard, as his focus was more on his skin being cooked, bringing all the silver to the surface, and finally cooling on top of him. It was starting to trap him in a prison of metal, making him into a giant statue. He twisted around, trying to escape his own skin, but there was nowhere to go.

He stood tall and tried to crawl away from this world and continued to scream as his movements slowed, and eventually stopped. Then, finally, quiet.

There was not much of the elixir left, but we had to try. Miss Cutty was able to salvage a bowl from her kitchen which we used to bring what we could find to Rebecca. A little could help, a lot was when it became a problem.

None of us loved the idea, but the other choice was worse. We tilted her head up to drink, and all watched. I wanted her to jump up, tell me how I had messed everything up, and have a laugh. That same laugh her father had.

"I think she's too far gone," Rose said.

Miss Cutty and I both looked at her, but neither of us had the strength to even agree or disagree. We just both made a face and waited.

"His mother was waiting, her arms spread out wide," a voice from behind me sang. "There was nowhere else Lumps wanted, but to be by her side."

I whirled around to see my mother, standing in what was left in the portal. I rushed over and reached out, and she took my hand.

"Mom! You made it back!"

Mom smiled as her head tilted to the side.

"I missed you," she said.

I threw my arms around her and she embraced me in return sending warm waves through my body. The empty space where my heart had gone missing felt full for the first time in ages. She looked the same as the night she vanished.

"I cannot believe it," I said. "You came back."

"I can't stay, sweetheart," she said.

I was weak, unable to even hold my arms up as I stepped back to look at her face. The fullness from before starting to leak out. A pinching in my chest made it hard to breathe.

"What?" I said. "Why?"

"This world does not work in that way," she said. "The Greedy One pulled others through, each time it burned his flesh, but it allowed him to absorb their life. But only three lives came through not pulled by him. Three came in, three can come back."

"That is perfect," I said, turning to Rose. "Right? Three in, three out. There was Boyd, Luther, and you."

Then I saw Miss Cutty, again, wringing the edges of her apron.

I turned back to see Mom. "Mom . . ." I said. "I just got you back." My hands started to shake and I clenched them in tight fists.

"You know the right answer," she said. "And if I was to return, then I return to what I knew before. Pain, fevers, blood."

"But I need you," I said. "I need you here with me."

"Sweetheart," she said. "I am with you."

She leaned out of the portal and embraced me again. Memories came back. Walking into town to help Mom with the shopping. Scraped knees. Mom and I in the kitchen. That stupid song. The blood. The cough. The darkness. It came back as I heard that familiar cough.

"You see?" she said. "There is no other answer."

Miss Cutty stepped forward. "I'm so sorry Ma'am, but does that mean my son is there?"

Mom stepped backwards into the portal as it made the slurping noise again and then fell still.

We all exchanged glances.

Rose stepped forward and rubbed her hand across my back, setting the tears loose as they fell down my cheek. She was right. I hated everything for it, but she was right.

I jumped as the portal spit out Luther, hand in hand with a small boy who looked like he was waking from a nap.

Miss Cutty screamed, "Joseph!" and jumped forward and lifted him into the air as she hugged him tight.

"I'm here too, Boss," Luther said. "No one missed me?"

"We all did," Rose said.

I looked behind Luther only to see the portal was gone. It had closed behind them just as Mom had said. Three in, three out. Even the pie was gone, which was likely for the best.

Luther saw me looking at the very empty space, as empty as I felt inside and put his arm around me.

"Your Mom's a great woman," he said. "She was the one who kept the kid and me safe. Kept us away from Boyd. She told me little Joseph reminded her of a little you. Her little Lump."

"She told you?"

"Something about the way things work there," he said. "I just sort of know."

I looked for the words to thank him, but—

"What happened to the asshole?" Rebecca said.

We all spun around to find Rebecca starting to sit up. She looked like hell, or maybe had just gotten back from it. She smacked her lips. "What's that awful taste?" Then it started to dawn on her. "Did you give me that damn elixir? Did you not learn anything?"

She glanced down at her arm. Still just the one.

"I admit, I was sort of hoping . . ." she said.

As our wagons started to pull out of Shadybrook, Rose and I considered what might be next for us. Maybe we could try our hand at magic. Rose was fast with the cards and since Luther had decided to stay with us for now, maybe he could be my assistant.

I did not know any tricks, but I did already have the hat.

It was a thought for another day.

Everything left of the elixir had gone up with the barn, and I would not have wanted it any other way.

I had decided to take one last stroll out in Jim Brown's pasture and grab the stone we found from before. I could not tell Rose about it. It felt a little wrong to have it. But, I liked having it to listen to. I held it to my ear.

"And that was the story, the story of Lumps. A story of someone, who got down in the dumps, who found his way back, from way out beyond, who discovered the love that he needed, was from his own pond."

184

THE END?

Not if you want to dive into more of the Dark Tide series.

Check out our amazing website and online store
or download our latest catalog here.
https://geni.us/CLPCatalog

Looking for award-winning Dark Fiction?
Download our latest catalog.

Includes our anthologies, novels, novellas, collections,
poetry, non-fiction, and specialty projects.

WHERE STORIES COME ALIVE!

We always have great new projects and content on the website to
dive into, as well as a newsletter, behind the scenes options,
social media platforms, our own dark fiction shared-world series
and our very own webstore. Our webstore even has categories
specifically for KU books, non-fiction, anthologies, and of course
more novels and novellas.

ABOUT THE AUTHORS

James Aquilone is the owner of Monstrous Books, writer of the *Dead Jack: Zombie Detective* series, and editor of the anthologies *Classic Monsters Unleashed, Shakespeare Unleashed*, and the 50th anniversary *Kolchak: The Night Stalker* graphic novel. He's won the Bram Stoker Award® for Best Graphic Novel, two Rondo Hatton Classic Horror Awards, and a Scribe Award from the International Association of Media Tie-In Writers. He's also been nominated for a Shirley Jackson Award.

Michael Knost is a two-time Bram Stoker Award®-winning editor and author of science fiction, fantasy, horror, western, and supernatural thrillers. He has written in various genres and helmed dozens of anthologies. His *Writers Workshop of Horror* won the 2009 Bram Stoker Award® in England for superior achievement in non-fiction. His *Writers Workshop of Horror 2* recently won the 2021 Bram Stoker Award® in Denver for the same category. His critically acclaimed *Writers Workshop of Science Fiction & Fantasy* is an Amazon #1 bestseller. *Return of the Mothman, Barbers and Beauties*, and *Author's Guide to Marketing with Teeth* were all finalists for the Bram Stoker Award®. Michael received the Horror Writers Association's Silver Hammer Award in 2015 for his work as the organization's mentorship chair and was recently recognized as the 2021 Mentor of the Year from the organization. He also received the prestigious J.U.G. (Just Uncommonly Good) Award from West Virginia Writer's Inc. His *Return of the Mothman* novel has recently been filmed as a movie adaption. He has taught writing classes and workshops at several colleges, conventions, online, and currently resides in Chapmanville, West Virginia with his wife, daughter, and a zombie goldfish.

Keith Lansdale writes comics, film scripts, novels, and short stories. Keith has made films such as *The Pale Door, The Projectionist* (in production), and *Christmas With The Dead,* adapted for the screen and the stage.

Keith has written multiple comics including *Hoot Goes There,* for *X-Files, Prisoner Of Violence, Crawling Sky, Vampirella,* and several others.

Among his writing credits are, the novel *Big Lizard* with Joe R Lansdale, as well as the short story, "Hoppity White Rabbit Done Broke Down", appearing in the recent collection: *The Drive-In: Multiplex.* As well as the story, "It Goes With Everything," found in the anthology, *About That Snowy Evening,* which Keith also co-edited.

Others of mention, soon to be released are *Elijah's Elixir,* a weird western, *Little Bird,* and more.

He co-edited *Son Of Retro Pulp Tales,* published by Subterranean Press.

Keith also co-wrote the children's story "The Companion" when he was twelve with his younger sister which was picked up by the tv show *Creepshow* and co-authored the children's book *In Waders From Mars.*

Readers . . .

Thank you for reading *Blood and Bullets*. We hope you enjoyed this 18th book in our Dark Tide series.

If you have a moment, please review *Blood and Bullets* at the store where you bought it.

Help other readers by telling them why you enjoyed this book. No need to write an in-depth discussion. Even a single sentence will be greatly appreciated. Reviews go a long way to helping a book sell, and is great for an author's career. It'll also help us to continue publishing quality books.

Thank you again for taking the time to journey with Crystal Lake Publishing.

Visit our Linktree page for a list of our social media platforms.
https://linktr.ee/CrystalLakePublishing

Follow us on Amazon:

MISSION STATEMENT:

Since its founding in August 2012, Crystal Lake Publishing has quickly become one of the world's leading publishers of Dark Fiction and Horror books. In 2023, Crystal Lake Publishing formed a part of Crystal Lake Entertainment, joining several other divisions, including Torrid Waters, Crystal Lake Comics, Crystal Lake Kids, and many more.

While we strive to present only the highest quality fiction and entertainment, we also endeavour to support authors along their writing journey. We offer our time and experience in non-fiction projects, as well as author mentoring and services, at competitive prices.

With several Bram Stoker Award wins and many other wins and nominations (including the HWA's Specialty Press Award), Crystal Lake Publishing puts integrity, honor, and respect at the forefront of our publishing operations.

We strive for each book and outreach program we spearhead to not only entertain and touch or comment on issues that affect our readers, but also to strengthen and support the Dark Fiction field and its authors.

Not only do we find and publish authors we believe are destined for greatness, but we strive to work with men and women who endeavour to be decent human beings who care more for others than themselves, while still being hard working, driven, and passionate artists and storytellers.

Crystal Lake Publishing is and will always be a beacon of what passion and dedication, combined with overwhelming teamwork and respect, can accomplish. We endeavour to know each and every one of our readers, while building personal relationships with our authors, reviewers, bloggers, podcasters, bookstores, and libraries.

We will be as trustworthy, forthright, and transparent as any business can be, while also keeping most of the headaches away from our authors, since it's our job to solve the problems so they can stay in a creative mind. Which of course also means paying our authors.

We do not just publish books, we present to you worlds within your world, doors within your mind, from talented authors who sacrifice so much for a moment of your time.

There are some amazing small presses out there, and through collaboration and open forums we will continue to support other presses in the goal of helping authors and showing the world what quality small presses are capable of accomplishing. No one wins when a small press goes down, so we will always be there to support hardworking, legitimate presses and their authors. We don't see Crystal Lake as the best press out there, but we will always strive to be the best, strive to be the most interactive and grateful, and even blessed press around. No matter what happens over time, we will also take our mission very seriously while appreciating where we are and enjoying the journey.

What do we offer our authors that they can't do for themselves through self-publishing?

We are big supporters of self-publishing (especially hybrid publishing), if done with care, patience, and planning. However, not every author has the time or inclination to do market research, advertise, and set up book launch strategies. Although a lot of authors are successful in doing it all, strong small presses will always be there for the authors who just want to do what they do best: write.

What we offer is experience, industry knowledge, contacts and trust built up over years. And due to our strong brand and trusting fanbase, every Crystal Lake Publishing book comes with weight of respect. In time our fans begin to trust our judgment and will try a new author purely based on our support of said author.

With each launch we strive to fine-tune our approach, learn from our mistakes, and increase our reach. We continue to assure our authors that we're here for them and that we'll carry the weight of the launch and dealing with third parties while they focus on their strengths—be it writing, interviews, blogs, signings, etc.

We also offer several mentoring packages to authors that include knowledge and skills they can use in both traditional and self-publishing endeavours.

We look forward to launching many new careers.

This is what we believe in. What we stand for. This will be our legacy.

**Welcome to Crystal Lake Publishing—
Tales from the Darkest Depths.**

9 781964 398242